I0636866

A Western Gentleman

Mike Gagnon

Published by Mike Gagnon, 2018.

A WESTERN GENTLEMAN

First edition. November 1, 2018.

Copyright © 2018 Mike Gagnon.

ISBN: 978-1988369266

Written by Mike Gagnon.

Chapter One

A dry tumbleweed rolled across the dusty desert plain, indifferently ambling over the emotionless face of an armadillo. The animal gave no response, parched and mummified as it was. What started as a simple search for food and drink on the open rock flats hadn't panned out, making the creature another victim of the harsh Arkansas sun. The oppressive waves of heat blasted the flat rocks, keeping in time with the slow, steady pulse of a horse and its rider. The horse was jet-black, save for the glistening sweat pulled forth by the sun. It made no mind or effort to dispute its lot in life or raise any kind of protest for its situation. The man atop the horse portrayed a mood as black as his steed, his fine jacket and bowler hat dark as well. His pale face held a neatly trimmed black handlebar mustache, waxed into perfect shape. He, too, made no protest about his situation despite the sweltering heat that he felt under his jacket.

The rider and his horse sauntered along the rocky plateau under the baking sun aiming for the shaded cover of a nearby river bank. Within thirty yards of it the cowboy and his horse approached a little ridge with a bluff. Small, scruffy bushes gripped the edge obscuring a small depression beyond the ridge from view. It was a minor detail, a drop of only a couple of feet. Nothing in and of itself presented any challenge to the rider's progress to the cool, green paradise in the distance.

As the rider approached the outcropping of sparse foliage there was a rustle, conveniently just out of view below the ridge. Now odds are, out in this country, the odd rustle could be as harmless as a prairie mouse. At worst, it could be a rattler. The thought of the latter was enough for the cowboy to rest his hand on the butt of his colt revolver. The fact that the rustle came from the one and only spot on the entire landscape that he couldn't see made him cautious enough to wrap his fingers around it. The rustle turned into a scuffle and slowly grew into the sounds of steel and leather, rock and hooves, clumsily scraping together in an inept ambush attempt. The rider slowly pulled his iron from its holster and rested it on top of his saddle horn in preparation. When the first gun muzzle appeared above the nearest bush along with the corner of a dirty, weather-beaten hat, a voice muttered to itself. The rider leveled his iron, aiming towards his would-be hijacker.

"Now hold on a minute, partner," came a greasy voice from under the hat. "That there is an act of hostility towards a man of the law."

A round, dirty face emerged from behind the bush. Filth and stubble blended together in a mottled, uneven tone. Large jowls shook under the ugly face. Carrying on the theme of dirt and stubble, he was covered with a thin layer of greasy sweat which caused him to glisten like a Christmas pig. His eyes were small, beady, and unnaturally close together; sunken and deep under a small, but pronounced brow ridge. Overall, his face looked as if it had shrunk somehow and been placed on a head two sizes too large. The muzzle of the rifle held tightly in his hands looked open toward the cloudless sky as if hoping for the blue expanse to give up some rain for its parched throat. Beige cowhide pants and pale blue shirt topped with black suspenders were visible under the man's open jacket. The jacket was a dark navy, or at least, after years of dust, dirt, and neglect, it made the worn and frayed garment look that dark; it could have been lighter. Beside the lapel, pinned over his heart was a tin star.

Behind him approached another man, equally dirty and greasy. This one was thin where the other was fat. He had the same beady eyes tucked under the same pronounced brow ridge, but the rest of his face was harsh and narrow with rat-like features. A bushy, unkempt mustache took up a quarter of the man's face; almost, but not quite hiding his pointed upper jaw. A severe overbite gave his mouth a gawkish, horse-like appearance. He wore a faded red shirt under blue suspenders that struggled to hold up a pair of denim coveralls that appeared several sizes too big for him. Over his trousers he wore a gun belt that held a shiny, seemingly expensive six-shooter on either side of him. They looked to be made of polished silver with mother-of-pearl handles. His right hand rested on the handle of his gun, ready to draw. The other hand held a leather strap, a bridle attached to a large mule being reluctantly pulled along. This man also wore a tin star pinned to his chest, matching his companion's.

"Begging your pardon, sir," the cowboy said. "No disrespect meant to the law. If you don't want to be greeted like bandits, you might not want to sneak up on a man like bandits. A fellow could get himself a dose of lead if he happened upon a stranger jumpier than me."

The lawmen were rustled, jumpy and indignant, the portly one lowering the muzzle of his rifle in self-defense.

"Was that a threat, mister, are you calling out the law?"

"Sure sounds like it to me, Leroy," the thin rat-faced lawman chimed in.

"Now hold on there, gents," the black-clad rider responded calmly. "I didn't intend to offend anyone or call anyone out. I'm simply telling the God's honest truth that it can be dangerous to sneak up on unsuspecting strangers."

"Cletus says you're calling me out, you calling my brother a liar? That's three charges then: threatening the law, trespassing, and insulting an officer," Rat Face added.

"Trespassing?" the rider replied indignantly. "That's crazy, this here is open territory. It ain't trespassing on land if it ain't owned."

"Sir, you're calling Cletus a liar again, so that's two counts of insulting an officer. You may not know the rules and borders around these parts, Mr. Fancy Pants, but Sheriff Behan says ignorance of the laws ain't no excuse for breaking them," dirty Leroy proclaimed confidently. "You see, stranger, this here is the town of Burlton, and the mayor of Burlton, he has declared the town closed to outsiders for the public safety."

"That's preposterous, sir," the lone rider replied. "Burlton is another ten miles east of here!"

"'Twas ten miles east of here up until about a year ago, smarty pants," Cletus, the rat faced deputy, responded with vehemence. He pressed his face within inches of the stranger. "The mayor done declared the town limits is now ten miles outside of the old limits in all directions, and that any outsider is to be considered trespassing on account of public safety."

"Is that so?" asked the black-clad stranger. "Y'all are closing off your town to people on the outside to keep you all protected. Is that it?"

Cletus looked at him with a sneer. "Yeah, you never know what kind of stranger is going to come in and pose all kinds of danger to our respectable townsfolk, so we'd rather have y'all strangers just stay away. We like to keep to ourselves. Y'all are violating the laws of our territory."

"Hush up," interrupted his round, dirty-faced companion. "This is what we're going to do: You've got some charges against you that you have to answer to now, so you're going to put that gun away and we're going to escort you into town. The sheriff and the judge can determine how severe your punishment is."

"Yeah, yeah, that's right," Cletus said. The narrow-faced lawman looked at his companion nervously, back and forth from him to the rider.

The stranger slowly returned his gun to his holster in compliance and raised his hands into the air.

"That's the smartest thing I've seen you do yet, Mr. Fancy Pants," said the fat, jowly lawman. "Now ride."

HOURS LATER THE TRIO rode into the town of Burlton. The two lawmen on donkeys kept their weapons aimed at the well-groomed stranger atop his horse. The stranger's hands gripped the bullhorn on his saddle with exhaustion as they slowly sauntered into town. The town looked dismal. The few people scattered among homes and stores nervously looked out their windows and watched the trio pass by. The buildings themselves looked like they hadn't been kept up in years. Paint peeled and wooden boards hung loosely on many of the buildings. The town looked anything but prosperous. Large tumbleweeds blew across the streets. A mangy, stray cat bolted across the dusty road and was soon followed by a thin, emaciated dog.

The trio slowly rode past the funeral home where a tall, gaunt man who appeared to be the undertaker stood in a black hat, grinning in a sickly manner. Nearby, a small funeral procession was leaving the building. Two horses and a wagon pulled a buggy with an open casket on it and came to rest on the side of the street for public viewing. Cletus rode up beside the stranger, kept his gun trained on him, looked at the casket, and then at the mysterious stranger.

"That there was an awful story. This is what happens when you try and cross the law in these parts."

"Cletus, shut it," said his rotund companion.

"No, no, Leroy, I do believe he needs to hear this. That fella right there, he was a dandy just like you. Same kind of hat, he was British though, he wasn't even from around here. He used to run that clothing store right over there. Now, my other brother, he took that over now on account that the owner's dead with no kin, but this man here, being left out on public display, there's a reason for that. Sad story, really. He tried to defame my dear father. My daddy is the mayor of this town, and this uppity British fellow, he started saying very disparaging things about him. Calling him a criminal, even! Can you imagine that? A former sheriff, now the mayor, accused of being an outlaw? Well, the people of Burlton didn't buy that story, not at all. Crazy fool. When he realized what he had done and that all the people in town continued to support my honorable father, well, he just couldn't live with the shame anymore and blew his own brains out."

"Cletus . . ." The man's jowly face shook as he shot him a glance of disapproval.

"Well that's all, stranger. Now you know what happens when someone around these parts tries to disparage the good people of Burlton."

The stranger's gaze left Leroy and Cletus and moved to the casket. He stared somberly for a moment before glancing back at the lawmen, his teeth tightly clenched. After another fifty yards, they approached the sheriffs' station. Cletus raised his gun into the air and fired it, getting the attention of townspeople.

"Fine people of Burlton, y'all hear this. We got ourselves an outsider trespassing in our fair town, and now he has been brought in. This is what happens to those who violate our laws." Leroy rolled his eyes and looked over at Cletus, but kept his shotgun leveled at the stranger. "This here gentleman has trespassed in our town, and he is now charged with multiple offenses. He is being charged with trespassing in our fair town as well as threatening the law, if you can believe that. And, insulting an officer!"

Leroy cleared his throat and chimed in, "Two counts of insulting an officer."

"Yeah, that's right," Cletus said. "Two counts of insulting an officer, and now he will be set to face judgment on these charges, witnessed by myself and my honorable brother, Leroy, deputy of this here fine town."

Throughout the speech several other deputies and an older, more distinguished gentleman in equally filthy, worn attire exited the sheriffs' station They all wore tin stars. It seemed obvious that the oldest man was the sheriff and the rest were his deputies. The sheriff looked at the stranger intensely and then spit a dark wad onto the dirt. He stared into the stranger's eyes.

"What do you say to these charges, stranger?"

The man on the horse looked at him innocently. "I do apologize, sir. I did not intend to offend anybody, and I did not know that I was trespassing."

"Ignorance of the law is not an excuse to disobey that law," the sheriff said loudly for his deputies and any townsfolk peering out windows and poking around outdoors to hear. "Dismount, sir." With that, the stranger raised his hands and slowly complied. "So, what say you to these charges?"

"I told you, sir, I didn't know. If people are unwelcome, you might think about doing the courteous thing of putting up a sign..."

"Again, ignorance of the law is no excuse for breaking the law. I'm going to have to ask you to release your gun belt until we have passed appropriate judgment on you. It is prohibited for any resident of Burlton to carry a firearm within the town limits unless they are a duly appointed officer of the law."

With the stranger's hands raised, Leroy nervously reached in and unbuckled the man's gun belt, being careful to keep his own gun trained on the stranger as he slowly slid the belt off. Cletus unstrapped the man's saddle and lifted it off his horse. The man's property was piled on the front porch of the sheriffs' station and his horse was tied to a post there.

"I'm afraid you are going to have to be held in a cell and your belongings will be held here until we can properly sentence you."

The stranger lowered his hands slightly, and looked up at the sheriff. "Now, sheriff, I do believe if you'll allow me, I can resolve this situation." With that, he slipped one hand into his jacket.

Cletus jumped and shouted, "He's reaching for an iron!"

All the lawmen simultaneously rushed to grab their weapons. Cletus fired, the bullet whizzing over the stranger's head. The stranger turned to Leroy and pushed his shotgun barrel to the sky with one hand and knocked out the portly lawman with the other.

Chapter Two

The stranger turned and lifted Leroy's shotgun into the air as it went off and knocked out the portly lawman with his free hand, then dove behind a nearby water trough. Bullets pelted the trough and caused the small holes to spring leaks and water to splash about. Cletus ran around the water trough to get a point-blank shot on the stranger. He stood over and sneered at the well-dressed man, giving the dandy enough time to forcefully kick Cletus in the leg, hooking his foot behind his knee which caused him to stumble to the ground and fire his gun off into the dirt. The stranger then grabbed Cletus' pistol from his fumbling hand and struck him squarely across the jaw, leaving him to roll in agony in the dirt.

Now that Cletus was clear, the other lawmen were eager to fire lead into the stranger without any further questions. Thinking quickly, the stranger dove behind the corner of a building as bullets tore at the wood siding inches away from him. The man stood with his back pressed against the building and called out to the lawmen as he gripped the pistol he'd swiped from Cletus and pointed it toward the sky.

"Now, gentlemen, hold on there. You can clearly see that I have procured a firearm from one of your fellow lawmen, and yet I have not fired back at you in hostility at all. Would you like to know why?"

From the front porch of the sheriff's station, the sheriff himself responded, "No one gives a fuck, you're a dead man!"

The sheriff then fired a shotgun, blowing the siding of the building apart and encouraging the stranger to run farther down the alley. As he rounded the corner, another lawman came at an equally fast pace around the next corner closely followed by another man wearing a tin star.

The stranger ducked as bullets began to perforate the wood of the back porch he was using for cover. He looked around and saw a chamber pot sitting atop a flat roof that covered the back porch of the building behind the two gunmen. The stranger quickly popped out from his cover and fired a shot, splintering the wood of the roof that had supported the pot, causing it to topple over and empty its contents onto a disgusted lawman who fell to the ground, rolling and screaming in disgust. The stranger ducked back down in time to avoid a bullet that was heading toward him from the other gunman. He gritted his teeth, took a deep breath, and then quickly stood, aimed, and fired off a bullet at the lawman, striking him in the hand and causing him to drop his weapon. The stranger then ran off around the building into the darkness.

The squad of lawmen spread out around the town, filling the streets and the alleys between the buildings. They uniformly held their guns at the ready, waiting to take on the stranger. One of the lawman called out to the sheriff.

"It's like he disappeared, like he was a ghost or something. He's just gone."

"He ain't gone, you idiot," the sheriff called back. "He ain't a ghost. He's a criminal who is going to be judged and executed by the law of this town."

"I just don't know where he could have gone," the lawman said in return.

The deputy failed to notice the stranger tucked up inside a porch roof, hanging several feet above his head. The stranger released his hold on the ceiling, landed on the lawmen's back, and caused him to stumble and fall flat on the ground. The lawman yelled in pain and his gun went off. The rest of his brethren began to close in, rushing towards the scene.

The stranger gripped the man's wrist tightly, forcing him to release hold of his long-barreled shotgun. The stranger grabbed the deputy's lapels and lifted the man to his feet, holding him in front of himself so that the eager officers of Burlton would hold their fire long enough for the stranger to speak. He was taking the gamble that they didn't want to turn their comrade into Swiss cheese in order to get retribution for the perceived disrespect they'd received.

The stranger called out: "Listen, there has been a misunderstanding and I can clearly explain why nobody needs to be executed or come to any harm today—"

In his desperation, the stranger had failed to notice another deputy sneaking up behind him. His voice was silenced in mid-sentence by a loud, painful thud; the butt of a shotgun colliding with the back of his head.

Chapter Three

The stranger felt an aching pain in the back of his head. As he slowly opened his eyes, his lids resisted the harsh light; it caused the throbbing pulse in his head to feel as if his skull was splitting open. He observed his surroundings with bleary eyes. He was held between two lawmen, one at each shoulder, on a bench in the front of a courtroom. A quick glance revealed that many of the lawmen, including the one who he had shot in the hand and the other who he had dumped a bucket of human waste on, were in the room along with Cletus and Leroy, bearing their own injuries. His glance also revealed that many townsfolk had come from hiding in their homes to fill the benches of a well-appointed courtroom. The people of town had somber expressions on their faces that didn't match the proud sneers held by their local law enforcement.

The gentleman stranger's gaze drifted up to the front of the room where a hefty man sat behind a podium. The man was clearly related to the sheriff—likely a brother but a little bit older and a lot fatter—and filled out a large black robe. It was obvious that he was the judge presiding over this courtroom. He looked down at the stranger and spoke.

"Well there, fancy stranger. Thank you for joining us. I am glad that you did regain consciousness so that you can see and be alert during final proceedings where we will read off your charges and rule on your sentencing. You sir, have violated the sanctity and peacefulness of the fair town of Burlton. In the process, you have been charged with trespassing, two counts of insultin' an officer, one count of threatening the law, three counts of out and out aggression towards the law, and two counts of attempted murder. What do you have to say for yourself, Mr. Stranger?"

Stuttering groggily the stranger responded, "Your . . . Your Honor, sir, I meant no one any disrespect, and when I attempted to explain before, your lawmen opened fire on me. I believe, if you look inside my jacket for the object I was reaching for when your men opened fire—I believe that all will be explained."

The judge looked at him skeptically, then nodded to the bailiff holding on to the stranger's left shoulder. The bailiff drew open the jacket and revealed a bronze star badge. Not just any star badge, but a badge that read *Marshal of the U.S. Federation*.

The lawmen that were near enough to see it, gasped. Cletus scurried over and looked at the badge, then looked up at the stranger, then turned to look at his kin sitting behind the bench.

"He, he's a Federal Marshal," Cletus said. The rat-faced deputy began to slink backward, still facing the stranger, a look of fear replacing the previous sneer of superiority he held. The judge looked down at the man.

"Now is that true, stranger? You're a U.S. Marshal?"

"Yes," the stranger replied. "My name is Lloyd Church Jr., U.S. Federal Marshal, and I'm traveling on business for the president himself. I represent President Lincoln, and have been given the duty to execute warrants on some of the most dangerous and wanted criminals in the federation. That's all I was trying to tell your men here before things got out of hand. I never meant any disrespect.

"Now, I'd like you to consider that I am willing to decline pressing my own charges of insulting an officer, and, as you put it 'threatening the law', if you are willing to drop yours. On account of the attempted murder and violence, I believe you'll find that had your men possessed calmer heads and allowed me to speak, we would not be in this situation. I would not have had to resort to any violence to defend myself. I believe that dropping or declining to press those charges I referred to, should outweigh the significance of the charges leveled against me, bearing in mind the fact that mine is of a federal jurisdiction."

There was a hush over the room. Now, the look on the spectators faces reversed. The stranger looked around the courtroom and saw a faint look of hope; there was just a tiny glimmer of optimism in their expressions. A few covered their faces to hide small curls of smiles, feeling they had to hide their pleasure. Now, the lawmen in the room looked nervously back and forth at each other and to the judge on the bench.

The judge looked down to the bailiff. "Remove the cuffs."

The bailiff complied and the judge glared at the marshal. "Marshal Church, if that be your name, we are going to come to a resolution. The town of Burlton concedes to delay any proceedings or charges until we can confirm that you are who you say you are. Until such time you will not leave the town limits, and if your identity is not verified, you will be back in this room facing prosecution. If your story does check out, we'll be happy to return your belongings including your horse, your saddle, and your firearms, and then you will be advised to make your way on through town. In the meantime, I will allow you to keep the firearm that you did obtain from Cletus, being as you are a man of the law. Make no mistake we will not tolerate any misuse of that firearm. There are many armed men in this room who would correct that situation if it does arise."

Cletus was dumbfounded. "What? What about . . . Why does he get to keep my firearm?"

The judge glared down at him. "Hush your mouth, boy. If you hadn't been an idiot he wouldn't have it in the first place." The judge turned to the stranger. "Please accept the apologies of our fair town, make yourself comfortable, and enjoy our hospitality until such time as we deem that you may go."

The judge continued to stare into the eyes of the marshal for several seconds after he finished speaking. The marshal returned the stare for an uncomfortably long time before the bailiff took a hint and pulled the marshal to his feet.

"All right then, Mr. Fancy Pants Marshal. You heard the judge, now get about your business." Turning to the audience the bailiff said, "And y'all keep quiet until we let you know it's okay to leave."

The judge turned and looked at the other bailiff, "Leroy, clear these people outta here."

Leroy waved his hands in the air, turned and yelled at the townspeople, "All right folks, all right, the hearing's over. There is nothing left to see here, there is nothing to see. Go on about your business. Get out. Court is no longer in session. Go on now. Get."

Cletus sheepishly crept towards the judge's bench as the court cleared out.

"Aww, Uncle Bob, why'd you have to go and let him keep my gun like that? That's embarrassing."

The large man leaving the bench turned and glared at his nephew. "Cletus, quit yer yammerin'. Soon enough you will have your firearm back, and his as well."

The marshal walked out of the courthouse a free man and looked down the streets of town, paying attention to where the citizens dispersed. He noticed a number of them heading over to a nearby saloon. The marshal wandered across the dusty street over to the saloon, ignoring the same stray cat as it ran by, followed by the emaciated dog continuing his hunt. As he opened the double saloon doors and walked in, the crowded room went from a low din to audible gasps. The stranger strode up to the bar and took a seat. He could see the saloon owner was a lanky and frail looking middle aged man with a large, bushy push-broom moustache in a pair of grey overalls over a blue shirt. His clothes looked like they should've been laundered more often than they were. The man was occupied in conversation with somebody else at the bar.

"Now, I can't afford no more insurance," the saloon owner said to the man at the bar. "I pay all I can as it is." The man at the bar tipped his hat and grinned.

"You know, Sam, what they say is that you can't afford *not* to have insurance. You never know what can happen. There might be a fire or a shooting or, God forbid, a fight breaks out and someone draws an iron and a stray bullet wounds and kills ya, leaving your family with quite a burden." Sam O'Hara looked at the man with a quiet intensity.

"All right, I'll do what I can, but you need to give me a couple more days."

"That's the spirit," the man said. "Where there's a will, there's a way, I always say." Sam hesitantly turned away from the insurance man to the stranger at his bar.

"What can I get you, stranger?"

"I'll just take a sarsaparilla," the marshal said. The insurance salesman looked down the bar at the marshal.

"Whoooeee! I heard about you, already! You're that fancy pants marshal from out of town. You sure did stir things up around here." The marshal turned to the man.

"I didn't come looking for attention. I came for a job. I do believe that it was your fine lawmen who brought the attention to me."

"Ha, ha, ha," the insurance salesman chuckled as he sauntered over to the marshal. "Well, that sounds a bit like tomayto-tomahto, right? Let me introduce myself. I do believe that you met my kinfolk earlier, many of them are the fine lawmen of this town. My name is

He stretched his hand out towards the marshal. The marshal looked at him for a moment and reluctantly extended his hand and shook it.

"Did you ever think about getting any insurance?" Jack Behan asked. "I provide the insurance around here to help protect fine establishments in Burlton such as this one, in the case of unfortunate and unexpected events. You can just never be too safe. I provide the insurance for all the folks around here, for property and for life, along with cattle and livestock."

"I bet you do a very brisk business," the marshal responded coolly.

"That I do, that I do, but I work hard for my money. Sometimes, it just takes a lot of convincing to get people to understand and realize just how valuable havin' insurance is. Isn't that right, Sam?" Sam gave

"Well, I do believe I'll be carrying on, marshal," Jack continued, "but it is nice to meet you, sir, and it has been a pleasure."

Without looking away from his drink the marshal replied, "I assure you, the pleasure has been all yours."

The insurance salesman was startled for a moment as he made his way towards the saloon doors. He froze, calculating his next move and how to respond.

"Ha, ha, ha. You are a funny one. You don't look it, but you are much funnier than I have been led to believe."

The insurance salesman nervously stumbled out the door. The marshal set his drink down and slapped two coins on the bar. Sam walked over, scooped the coins up and put them into his pocket.

"Can I get you anything else, marshal?" the bartender asked.

"No, Sam. I do think I've gotten what I needed here."

The marshal then rose to his feet and sauntered out of the saloon. Marshal Church gazed across the street at a group of grungy-looking men—some wearing tin stars and some not—intoxicated, laughing, and carrying on in the street indecently in front of the brothel with a couple ladies of the night. He stood and thought for a minute, then turned around and walked back into the saloon. He approached the bar and reached inside of his jacket, pulled out a bag of coins from his pocket, and tossed it on the bar.

"Hey, Sam?" he asked. "You got a room to let in here?"

Chapter Four

M arshal Church, as people now knew him, dimmed the gas lamp on the dresser of the small room he'd rented above the saloon. He took off his jacket and uniform and hung them on the coat rack next to the door. He slipped the gun belt holding Cletus's revolver back on over his long johns and gently lowered himself on to the bed. Keeping the gun with him was an obvious sign of unease and distrust of the town folk, and the lawmen in general. The time he had spent riding, being escorted into town, and the subsequent gunfight and hearing had taken its toll on him and he soon drifted off to sleep.

It wasn't long before his mind conjured images of a former time. A time in his youth, fifteen years earlier. He pictured the small, humble home in the desert, roughly a mile outside of town. He was ten, playing with a wooden horse and buggy on the floor. His father, a dapper gentleman, wore a black cowboy hat, a clean shirt, a dusty pair of brown chaps, and a gun belt that held two beautiful mother-of-pearl handled six shooters. Over his shirt, he wore a black vest with a prominent tin star that said "Sheriff" pinned above his heart.

HE GRINNED FROM BENEATH an upturned mustache and approached his beautiful wife who was working at the open fireplace making dinner for her family. He snuck up behind her and nibbled on her ear.

"Stop it, Lloyd," she giggled. "Not in front of the kids."

The man chuckled, "Oh hell, Isabelle, before you know it we're going to have to be explaining this to them anyway. Hmm. I ain't never heard of no kids turning into outlaws by growing up in a family full of love, anyway."

"Just stop it, Lloyd," Isabelle chided. "Dinner will be ready soon then you can get a good night's rest and get back to hunting bandits and such."

"Ha," Lloyd chuckled again, "don't see too many bandits around these parts anyway. Most I ever deal with is somebody lettin' their cattle loose or failing to fence them in and having them eatin' the neighbor's crops. I don't think we've had an arrest here in the last three years."

Isabelle smiled, "That's because the town has such a good sheriff."

"Oh, I just think maybe people in town are decent folk and know how to conduct themselves in a civilized manner."

Lloyd Junior overheard the conversation from the living room and called out to his father.

"Pa, are you sure we're safe from bandits?"

"Son," the sheriff chuckled, "I think we're 'bout as safe from bandits as a person can be in this world."

Lloyd Junior left his toys and walked into the kitchen.

"Are you sure, Pa? 'Cause when I saw Nancy DeLacey at Sunday school she told me she heard tell that there was a gang, the Shannon gang, seen heading this way. I hear they're a real bad bunch of ornery outlaws and bandits." Isabelle looked concernedly at her son and then her husband.

"Well, son," the sheriff said confidently, "this town here is a town of law and order, and Nancy DeLacey is most likely just telling yarns. The Shannon gang are probably heading way off out of here, likely to Mexico. There are so many people hunting for them, I hear tell even the cavalry is after them. They're going to be heading out of these United States and gonna be looking to hide out in Mexico, where they'll probably meet their end."

Isabelle looked anxiously from her husband to her son. "Lloyd, we're perfectly fine and safe here in this town as long as your pa is sheriff," she said reassuringly.

Little Lloyd said, "Yeah, my pa is the best sheriff ever." The boy smiled and stuck two fingers in the air as if firing guns. "Pew, pew, pew, pew!"

Lloyd Senior leaned forward and ruffled the young scamp's hair. "You betcha, but ya know, being a sheriff has a lot more to do with being able to talk to people and communicate with them, than with firing a gun. You know I always tell you that, right?"

"Yes, Pa, I know," Lloyd Junior responded, "but sometimes you just gotta shoot them outlaws. Pew, pew!"

"What kind of nonsense is that silly boy talking now?" asked a voice from the doorway. It was Camille, Lloyd Junior's older sister. She was budding into a beautiful young woman. Five years older than Lloyd, she recently celebrated her fifteenth birthday and was getting to the age where she'd soon be courting gentlemen from town. Lloyd Senior seriously worried about this and about his little girl becoming a woman.

"I see you're back," said Isabelle. "How was the social in town?"

"It was great," said Camille, smiling.

"Really? Great? A social? Last time you went to one, you said it was, what was it? 'Dull enough to dry molasses.' Wasn't that how you described it?"

Camille looked at her mother shyly. "Yes, but this time John Pennyworth was there."

Lloyd Senior turned quickly and looked at her.

"Oh, John Pennyworth, is it?"

"Yes," Camille sighed happily.

"Isn't his father the one that runs the horse and cattle dealership?"

"Yes," said Camille, brightening.

Isabelle, showing some interest, smirked. "And what's so interesting about Mr. Pennyworth?"

"Well, he asked if I could go to the play with him next week," said Camille. "He wants to know if he can court me."

"Courtin' now, is it?" asked Lloyd with concern. "Not sure you're old enough for that."

"Stop it, Lloyd," Isabelle interrupted. "You know she is becoming a woman, and I think she will do very well. She could do much worse than to be courted by a young Pennyworth."

"So, can I go courtin', Pa?" Camille asked hopefully.

"Well, let's hold on, this hasn't been discussed completely yet." Lloyd sat down, contemplating this new, worrisome development.

"I would be happy to chaperone you." Isabelle said, giving Lloyd a stern glare. Lloyd sat in silence for a moment.

"All right, if your momma's gonna chaperone, you can go" her father conceded reluctantly. Camille jumped up, giddy with excitement.

"Oh, thank you, thank you, Pa!" She planted a kiss on his cheek.

"Courtin'? Who wants to do that?" asked little Lloyd. "Too many bad guys to rustle."

Lloyd Senior laughed, "Well now, you may not always feel that way, young Lloyd."

"I doubt it," Lloyd Junior said. "I wanna be a wild west roper and I wanna be sheriff just like you, Pa."

Lloyd Senior chuckled. "Well, that may very well be if you follow a good example, son. Don't get carried away now, but I don't know, seems to me like you got an awful lot of interest in that Nancy DeLacey."

Lloyd Junior blushed, "Yeah, she's all right, for a girl," he said quietly. He then resumed his imaginary gunplay.

"Pew, pew, pew, pew!" he gestured with his fingers in the air and returned to his toys in the living room.

A few hours later the family, full of dinner, sat together in the living room, cozy in their night clothes, almost ready for bed. Young Lloyd was drifting off and let out a yawn.

"Well, it's about time for you to get to bed," Isabelle said.

"Yes, momma," he said reluctantly and set down a small chap

"Well, you can read all about it tomorrow," she said. "You children head off to bed now."

JUST AS LLOYD JUNIOR was dozing off, he heard the distinct crack of a riding crop. Then, voices giving commands to their horses.

"Yah, yah!"

They were foreign voices; not the voice of his father. A glow came in through the window above his bed and he saw the shadow of a man on horseback go by.

"Pa?" he called out. "Ma?" Fearfully, Lloyd Junior climbed out of bed.

"There's somebody outside, Pa!" He rushed into the kitchen where he saw his mother and sister huddled together nervously.

"Hush now, Lloyd," Isabelle said sternly, motioning for him to join them. "Your pa is going to check out what's going on."

Lloyd Senior crept from a side entrance across the darkened porch to see a group of men circling the house. Some of them carried torches, others had shotguns or pistols propped on the bull

"Are you sure this is the place?"

Through the light of the torches, Lloyd glimpsed the faces of the two men who whispered in the night. Immediately, he crept back through the doorway and closed it behind him, turning to face his family in the kitchen. Eyes wide in disbelief, he looked at his wife and addressed her in a serious tone.

"It's the Shannon's!" he said as quietly as he could although alarmed. Camille was suddenly overcome with fright and choked back a sob.

"Hush now," Isabelle consoled, "everything's going to be all right."

"You and the kids get in the back," Lloyd Senior said. "I will take care of this." Isabelle quickly ushered her children into the back room of the house.

"What are we so worried for?" Lloyd Junior asked. "Pa is going to shoot those outlaws."

"Hush now Lloyd, you need to be quiet, all right?" Isabelle said crossly. "You don't talk like that, and right now you don't talk at all, you gotta be as quiet as a church mouse and we're going to stay back here, okay?"

Moments later footsteps were heard on the front porch of the Church residence, along with a loud banging knock on the front door. It echoed through their home and was the loudest knock Lloyd had ever heard. The sound seemed to reverberate through the doors, beams, and plaster of the house. Lloyd took a deep breath, approached the door and gently turned the handle, opening it just a crack. A gruff, stubbly face appeared on the other side lit by the glow of nearby torches. Lloyd recognized the man as Wilfred Shannon, head of the Shannon gang; the bandits that Nancy DeLacey told Lloyd Junior about. The face looked grimly at Lloyd.

"Are you Sheriff Church?"

"That I am," Lloyd said through the small opening of the door.

"Well, Sheriff Church, I need to report a crime."

"Well I do appreciate that sir, but you can see I'm at home resting after a long day. So, if it isn't so urgent, maybe you could be so kind to come by the station tomorrow morning and I'd be happy to take your report then." Lloyd was quite diplomatic under the circumstances.

"Well, it can't wait, sheriff." said the bandit at his door. "See, I need to report a murder."

Sheriff Church worked hard to maintain his composure and showed no sign that he recognized the man.

"All right then, sir. What is the murder you need to report?" Lloyd asked patiently. Wilfred Shannon responded to him quietly.

"As a matter of fact, this one."

A bullet fired. Wilfred Shannon had soundlessly slipped his gun out of his holster during the conversation and had slowly pointed it at the sheriff's waist. The bullet tore through Lloyd's stomach and knocked him away from the door, allowing the outlaw to kick it open. The members of his gang rushed in. Wilfred Shannon laughed cruelly while Lloyd's family fearfully huddled in the back of the house and heard all that was transpiring.

"You see, Sheriff, well, we're outlaws, and we don't wanna deal with the law. We decided we'd like to stay around this town for a while. Well, we'd just like to not be bothered."

With that Wilfred Shannon fired another shot that narrowly missed the sheriff. Lloyd drew his gun, and through the growing haze of shock from his stomach wound, fired a bullet over his attackers left shoulder, directly through the skull of one of the gang members behind him. Blood splattered all over the top of the door frame behind him.

"Well shit," said Wilfred, "that was my cousin."

He fired another bullet into Sheriff Church's body. Lloyd, with two bullets in him, struggled to get up to defend himself as the Shannon gang surrounded him and crowded into the kitchen. In the back room, Isabelle looked intently at her children.

"You stay out of sight. You hide somewhere until this is done." Isabelle ran into the room as tears welled up in her eyes and hoped she could reason with the gang.

"You all can just leave, you just leave right now. We won't bother you at all." In response, the man over Wilfred's right shoulder raised his gun and fired point blank into Isabelle's mouth sending her body collapsing to the floor. Wilfred looked down at Lloyd coldly as he slouched on the floor holding his bleeding belly closed with his hand.

With dead eyes Wilfred whispered, "One of yours for one of ours."

Lloyd stared at the body of his wife dying on the floor in disbelief and shock. Tears welled up in his eyes and rage filled his heart. In great pain, he slowly pulled himself up the wall and gritted his teeth as the gang looked at him with ruthless grins. He raised the pistol and pointed it at Wilfred Shannon, but before he could fire off a shot, several gang members opened fire on Lloyd. Bullets tore through Sheriff Church's body and the walls behind him. Seconds later he collapsed dead on the floor next to his wife. The children cried in the back room, having heard everything.

Camille turned to her brother, "Listen, we gotta get into the bedroom. We're going to go into the bedroom and you're going to hide under the bed. We're going to hide and we're gonna be fine. We're going to wait until they leave, understand?" Lloyd nodded.

Camille hurried her brother into the bedroom and he hid under the bed. The Shannon's heard the shuffle of feet from the kitchen. Cletus Shannon turned to his father, Wilfred.

"I hear something going on back there, we best check it out."

Before Camille had been able to find an appropriate hiding place for herself, the outlaws kicked the bedroom door open with guns drawn. Wiping the tears from her face and putting on a brave front, Camille turned to face her assailants.

"What do y'all want? Camille demanded.

"Oh, well, aren't you a tiger!" Cletus exclaimed, amused. "Well, you all alone here, missy, now that your folks are dead? You don't have any other family here, now do you?"

"No, I'm the only one," Camille lied, looking at the ceiling. She refused to meet his eyes as a hot tear betrayed her and rolled down her cheek.

"Well now, I guess that means that you and me, we could have us some fun."

"Well, I'd like to have me some fun first," said Allister Shannon, Cletus's father and Wilfred's brother. "And since I'm older, I get to go first."

"Ah, shucks," said Cletus, disappointed. "You always gota ruin mah fun, Pa."

Allister drew his gun and pointed it point blank under the chin of Camille Church.

"Now, you just do what I say and co-operate honey, and you gonna be just fine." Allister loosened his gun belt and dropped his pants to the floor. Camille didn't respond, she just stared at the ceiling as sobs began to escape.

"Oh, now honey, I promise this ain't gonna hurt too bad, but don't think I'ma stop 'cause your cryin'. That's just makin' me more prepared. Gettin' me ready." Allister gripped the fabric of Camille's nightgown and ripped it off exposing her body. He pressed his gun under her chin, forced her bak and shoved her onto the bed. Lloyd recalled his sister's words to stay hidden although he could hear the man on the bed with his sister, violating her. The creaking of the mattress springs along with Camille's screams, gasps, and sobs filled the air while the other men watched gleefully, whooping and whistling. After several minutes Allister released a moan of pleasure.

"You did good darlin'." Camille responded by continuing to sob. Allister got up from the bed, put his pants on, and looked back at Camille on the bed.

"Ah look at this, y'all not wanna get involved in this. She's ruined. She just ain't got the mental fortitude to handle being a woman." He turned and fired two bullets through Camille's chest. The bullets ripped through the bed right above Lloyd's head and into the floor. He gripped a loose floorboard as tears ran down his cheeks. He looked at the holes made by the bullets that had just killed his sister. Her blood slowly began to soak the mattress above his head.

"Ah, shit!" Cletus barked. "Way to go and ruin it for the rest of us!"

Allister chuckled and left the room. The rest of the gang followed him save one. He stood and looked at the lifeless body of Camille Church stripped naked on the bed.

"Ah hell, there's enough of her left for ol' George."

The outlaw dropped his pants, climbed onto the bed, and began to violate the lifeless body. As George began to thrust into her and moan loudly, Lloyd looked at the gun belt on the floor. He trembled frantically as he reached out his hand; it shook uncontrollably almost to the point of being useless. Slowly and gingerly he began to loosen one of the six-shooters from George's belt. Just as he had loosened the gun he heard footsteps. He quickly pulled the six-shooter under the bed with him. Cletus came to the doorway and saw his fellow outlaw having sex with a dead girl.

"Oh George, you're doing that again? Jesus, you could've at least closed the door this time."

"Christ now, Cletus, it's going to take me another minute or two to finish."

"Well, just hurry up, we got us a town to take care of. We got things to do now that we got the law out of the way."

"Cletus Behan! Just get the hell out of here!"

Suddenly the thrusting motion above the bed became faster and more forceful. It caused the red stain on the bottom of the mattress to grow rapidly. Moments later George let out a loud sigh of pleasure.

"Oh, that was good, girly. You do it just the way I like it." He rose up from the floor and put his pants on. Absentmindedly, he failed to notice the gun missing from his holster. As he left the room with his back turned, his silhouette was perfectly lit in the doorway. Lloyd pointed the six-shooter directly at the man's back and pulled the trigger.

Click.

The gun had already been emptied into his father and there were no live bullets left in the chamber. As he exited the room, George thought he heard a noise and turned back to look over his shoulder. Seeing nothing, he left.

Lloyd tossed the useless gun aside. A moment later George came back, his steps quickening as he approached. "Now where the hell did I leave my other gun?" George mumbled to himself. He walked into the room and the light that shone in revealed the gun laying in the middle of the floor. "Oh hell, how did I miss that before? Jeeze."

George bent over just a few feet away from Lloyd's face and picked up the gun. Lloyd held his breath and stifled his sobs long enough to go unnoticed as George stood and placed the gun back in its holster.

"Jesus, I gotta stop doing that or Wilfred's going to shoot me himself," George muttered as he left the room.

The gang ransacked the kitchen for supplies and found coffee, dried fruit, and beef. They took what was useful and went outside. As they stood on the front porch Cletus turned to Wilfred.

"What do you want to do with the house? There ain't no one here no more." Wilfred looked back at him and smiled.

"My boy, we gonna have any house we want. We gonna build any house we want. Something much fancier and nicer than this one and no one's gonna stop us. Torch it." Two of the outlaws threw their torches in through the windows and the kitchen was soon ablaze. The men mounted their horses and rode off toward town.

Smoke began to fill the house as young Lloyd crawled out from under the bed. There seemed very little chance of escape. Lloyd ran to the back room, grabbed a chair and smashed the window. He stood on the chair and jumped out, hitting the dusty ground with a thud. As the house erupted into flames that lit up the night, Lloyd crawled a good thirty yards in sand and dirt until he was out of energy. He couldn't hold back the rush of emotions any longer and buried his face and arms in a sand dune. Lloyd Jr. sobbed pitifully until he had sobbed out every ounce of strength left in his body. Exhausted, he fell asleep in the early light of the desert morning.

Chapter Five

Marshal Church bolted upright in bed shocked, awake, alert, and sweating heavily. It had been a long time since Lloyd Junior had been troubled by dreams of what happened to his family. The morning light shone through the window and Marshal Church wiped the sweat from his face. He rose from the bed and used the wash

The saloon was quiet with only a couple of patrons hanging around. Sam was cleaning up blood and broken glass from fights the night before. A couple of drunks had already staggered in and were drinking their breakfasts. The marshal nodded at Sam and walked out onto the dusty street, took a deep breath and walked toward the diner. It was visible from the front step of the saloon like most of the stores in town.

As he entered the diner he removed his hat. A quick sideways glance revealed that he had caught the attention of the sheriff who was enjoying an oatmeal breakfast with several other "distinguished" members of Burlton. The mayor, the real estate agent, the landlord; all family members and relations in some way or another. Brothers, nephews, cousins, or close family friends of the Behan clan. The marshal approached the counter. The lady behind the counter eyed him up and down before speaking.

"What can I get you, mister?"

"Well, I think I'll just have oatmeal."

"Good, cause that's about all we got," she said.

"Well then, I'm much obliged, ma'am. I'll take a coffee too, if you got any of that."

"You're in luck, mister, I think you just about covered our menu."

The marshal chuckled and dropped a shiny coin on the counter. The woman brought a thick bowl of oatmeal and a dark cup of coffee. The marshal tipped his head to her as if he was tipping his hat, took a long sip of his coffee, and subtly looked over his shoulder at the table of men staring at him. He couldn't help but notice they all still had their hats on.

"Yeah, that there's the feller who says he's a Federal Marshal and caused all the ruckus yesterday," the voice of Sheriff Zachariah Behan said quite loudly.

Marshal Church turned in his seat and looked at the table full of men.

"I do believe I heard my name, sir," the marshal said. "I guess that means introductions are in order." The marshal left his breakfast behind and held his hat as he sauntered over to the table. "Pleasure to see you again, Sheriff Behan. Hopefully, there's no hard feelings."

The sheriff grumbled as the marshal extended a hand to shake.

"No," sheriff Behan responded.

The sheriff looked at the extended hand with a scowl and a humph. Next to him the insurance salesman, James Behan, chuckled and reached out, taking the marshal's hand.

"Well marshal, it's good to see you again. I do hope you thought about that insurance we talked about before," he said. The insurance salesman looked with a grin back and forth at the men sitting at the table.

"I appreciate that offer sir, but, you know, I do feel that I may not be here long enough to be in need of your insurance." The sheriff looked at the marshal through his scowl.

"You got that right." The marshal made eye contact with him but chose to ignore the comment.

"And who are these fine gentlemen?" the marshal asked politely. Another rotund man lifted a hand and nodded to the marshal.

"Well, I'm the sheriff's brother, Allister Behan, the mayor of this town."

"Mayor Behan," the marshal replied pleasantly.

"I don't want to say it's a pleasure to meet ya because you have made such a ruckus and apparently upset my brother here, but I will shake your hand all the same, only on account of you're a man the law, as you say."

"Well, I appreciate your civility Mayor Behan and I dare say you will soon have confirmation of my identity." The fourth man who had yet to be introduced spoke.

"Oh, that is correct, it will be," said the man. The unidentified man reached out and took the hand of the marshal for a quick shake.

"Nice to make your acquaintance and all that. I'm Doctor McCoolie, the town doctor, as well as the druggist here. The telegraph is in my dispensary down the street yonder, and well, we rushed out a telegram yesterday over the wires. We shall expect a confirmation as to your claim one way or the other very soon."

"Well, I appreciate that, Doctor McCoolie. Pleasure to meet you and make your acquaintance.' the marshal said.

Marshal Church was doing a very good job pretending not to notice the feigned respect he was receiving from the men. As his attention turned back to the sheriff, the town of Burlton's head lawman took his hand and finally shook it. The dirty and gruff man leaned forward, close to the marshal.

"Well, marshal, we will know soon enough and you best hope that your story is true, 'cause if it's not, you will be right back in that courtroom," the sheriff said. "Now we do not look kindly on people who shoot our lawmen and offend the fair people of our town, regardless of whether they are the law or not." The marshal squeezed the sheriff's hand tightly before breaking his grip and grinned, looking down at the men and back at the sheriff.

"Well, as a fellow man of the law I do appreciate your feelings and as I've said, I have apologized as best I can for the misunderstandings that we've had. I assure you gentlemen, when my identity is cleared, we will be able to put this situation behind us." The marshal then grunted and walked toward the door. He lifted his hat into the air and looked back at the woman behind the counter.

"Thank you very much for the wonderful breakfast, ma'am." Marshal Church placed his hat back on his head as he walked out the door. He looked back at the roundtable of skeptical glares directed at him.

"I do hope you fine gentleman have an enjoyable day," he said.

The marshal squinted as he walked back out into the harsh desert sun. He strode about thirty yards down the street and entered the town's bank. A familiar hush and murmur filled the bank. Patrons and staff members turned and spoke to a man seated at the desk behind a tall counter with barred windows. The man rose as he looked at the marshal. The man seemed to be in charge and watched the marshal wait his turn in line. When a young teller motioned Marshal Church to approach, the man that had been watching him waved the teller out of the way and took his place.

The marshal stepped forward and with a grin said, "Good day."

The banker responded curtly. "A good day to you too, sir. Well, I know everyone in this town and I don't recognize you, so you must be that new marshal causing such a stir."

Marshal Church grinned. "Yes, I guess that would be me. Does my reputation precede me?"

The banker responded very indignantly, "I believe sir, if that were accurate you would be mistaking reputation for infamy."

The marshal chuckled. "You know, the funny thing is that I continue to apologize to everyone of stature in this town and I seem to be rebuked consistently."

The banker glowered at him. "Well, maybe you're rebuked because your conduct has so upset the citizens of Burlton."

The marshal grinned again. "Well shoot, let me try and make a new introduction and start off on the right foot." He extended his hand through the bars. "I am Marshal Church."

The banker hesitantly reached out and shook his hand.

"Ezekiel George, sir."

The marshal held the man's grip firmly. "It's a pleasure, sir." In response the banker sneered, still gripping his hand.

"Oh, I assure you, the pleasure is all yours." The marshal tightened his grip on the banker's hand and chuckled.

"Oh, so I guess you must know that insurance salesman. Word got around, did it?"

"Yes, the Behan's are close family acquaintances going back many years and for many generations in my family, and we don't like comments and disrespect to our friends and family, now do we, Mister Church?"

"Marshal. Marshal Church." The marshal still clasped the banker's hand firmly.

"Oh, my apologies, *Marshal* Church," the banker said in mild mockery. "What brings you into my fine establishment today . . . Marshal Church?"

The marshal gripped the banker's hand tighter and brought his own hand closer to his body, pulling the banker forward so his face was uncomfortably close to the bars.

"Well, once I'm done waiting for your friends, the Behan's, to confirm my identity, I'll be back to my work filling out warrants for the U.S. government. I may very well find a bandit or a wanted outlaw somewhere in this region, and if I do, I want to know if your sheriff's office has enough on hand to fill the bounties on those warrants."

The banker then became nervous but looked the marshal in the eye.

"The sheriff's office can cover whatever debts it has, but I don't believe you're gonna find any criminals here in Burlton."

"Never said I was," said the marshal. "But let's say I get twenty miles or I should say, ten miles now, outside of the town limits and I find a rustler in the desert?"

The banker looked at him, narrowing his eyes in a hard glare. "What are you sir, a marshal or a bounty hunter?" The marshal took a breath in and grinned over clenched teeth.

"Well sir, I am a marshal, but I do believe in accordance with the laws of the land, that any such person who does apprehend a criminal with a bounty, lawman or not, is eligible to collect upon that reward as set aside by the federal funding of the law."

The banker gritted his teeth and pulled his hand away trying not to shake off the pain. The marshals' grip had become much tighter than he realized.

"Well, yes sir," the banker said, now clenching his teeth. "I assure you that our law is able to cover any debts with the funding available." The banker raised his voice with the last few words. The marshal grinned and tipped his hat to the banker.

"Thank you for confirming that, sir, that was my only inquiry. I appreciate you taking the time, Mr. George." Despite himself, the banker rubbed the knuckles of his right hand.

"Much obliged," the banker said.

The marshal turned and strolled out of the bank. He strolled down the street inspecting the town, until he passed by the corpse still lying on the side of the street in a coffin. He looked at it somberly and then up at the caretaker's office. A tall, lean gentleman in a fine, high black hat came out. He greeted the marshal, extending a hand and leaned over. His tall frame towered over the marshal especially as he was standing two steps above him.

"Well hello, good sir," the undertaker said. The marshal shook his hand, getting up into his face.

"You're the undertaker around these parts, I take it?" asked the marshal.

"Yes, I am, yes I am. I do serve this town and it looks like you have made the acquaintance of our local bank."

"I sure did. Interesting take on hospitality," the marshal remarked, unimpressed.

The Undertaker laughed.

"Oh, he can't even help it, he can't help it. Please do not hold it against my dear brother, Zeke. He gets very stressed, managing things like the money for all the townsfolk. You know, so much to handle, so little time. It gives him an awful case of the sweats some days." The marshal looked at the undertaker, puzzled.

"The banker is your brother?"

"Sure, he is, he is. The pride and joy of my momma an' poppa," he said. "Yeah, that's my brother Zeke. I took a different path. My name is Gallant, Mr. Gallant George."

"Well, I appreciate that, Mr. George. Tell me, is everybody in this town related?" The Undertaker chuckled.

"No, but well, you know we're all the same in the hereafter." The Undertaker gestured towards the corpse, grinning at his own morbid joke.

"I see," said the marshal. The smile fell from his face, replaced with disgust.

"Yes, marshal, our family, the Georges, have been a fine, upstanding part of the community and close friends of the Behan's for many years. We all worked together to make sure Burlton is a safe and honorable community." The marshal looked up at the undertaker.

"Gallant George . . . and that'd include not allowing strangers in the town?"

"Oh, that might be a big part of it," the undertaker said. "You know, it was many a year ago some unruly bandits came in, and well, they terrorized this town. Strangers came in and terrorized this town and they even shot the sheriff."

The marshal winced and looked at him through slanted eyes. "Is that so?"

"That's so, but that was how we bonded together. The Georges and the Behans, and my dear friend, Mayor Allister Behan; he stood up and he replaced that sheriff to help protect the people of Burlton, and since then, we've prospered. We've done very well because of the bravery and leadership of Mr. Allister Behan, we owe him a lot."

"Sounds like you're ready to saint him," said the marshal.

"Oh, well, no, that's a job for a different family member, Allister's younger brother, Josiah. He's always followed that righteous path and he does lead his flock like nobody else." Mr. George looked down the street toward the church. "He too, found the Lord's calling after the town's previous pastor had met an unfortunate and untimely end. Horse gave out to the next town over and well, it was weeks before we found him dried out in the desert. That was a difficult burial, difficult body preparation, let me tell you," murmured the Undertaker, lost in thought. The marshal couldn't hide the revulsion on his face.

"Well, I'm sure you would know."

"That I would," said the undertaker.

"Pleasure to make your acquaintance."

"Marshal, I do have to carry on with some business," he gestured again to the corpse. The marshal's curiosity was piqued and he turned to inquire of the undertaker.

"Tell me something, sir, do you always leave the bodies of the dead exposed like this in the street?"

"Oh, well now that is a different story," the man said. "You're a stranger. Normally, I'd say that strangers are not concerned about the affairs of our town, but well, this is a special case, you know. This man committed some great disrespects to our fair people and our mayor, and tried to make a number of accusations. Scandal, I say, scandal!

More scandal than this town has seen in a while. Unfortunately, the man could not handle that the fine people of Burlton did not support him, and he took his own life. So, we leave him on display as a reminder to people of what happens when you besmirch our fine town, and also on account of taking your own life and condemning your soul to hell. Serves as a good, somber reminder to the rest of our upstanding citizens."

"Yeah, the sheriff's nephew Cletus informed me of that when he marched me into town at gunpoint."

The Undertaker chuckled. "Well then, I guess I'm not giving you much information...unless he told you the rest."

"What's that?" asked the marshal.

"Well, rumor has it, well, this man would've burned in hell, anyway whether he had taken his own life or not. They said that he kept a child out on his farm. See, he lived way out in the desert, he had the clothing store in town here, but for some reason he preferred to live out there with the coyotes and the cactuses. Well, they said that he kept a boy and was buggering him. Imagine that, buggerin' on a boy? Deviant behavior, I'd say."

"Sure would, if you could prove some sort of accusation like that," the marshal said with skepticism.

"Well, you know that's the problem. Now, we heard for years he was buggering the young boy out there. Other people hanging out there, too, but that boy up and disappeared. We figured that deviant there just got rid of him somewhere out in the desert. His soul was damned long before he ever caused a fuss here in town." The marshal looked at him intensely.

"Anyone ever have any proof of that? Any evidence?"

The Undertaker looked at him skeptically. "We don't need no evidence for that kind of aberration."

The marshal looked at the Undertaker sternly. "Well, it seems to me if you're all such fine, upstanding, peaceful and law-abiding citizens, and you knew about such a crime going on, wouldn't you have investigated and laid charges?"

The Undertaker looked at him, disbelief on his face turning into incredulity. "Well, sir, I do believe when someone is committing such violent, disgusting acts like that, which made our finest folk shrink up so much on account of the unspeakable sins, and that they thought such a charge to be so damning, they wanted to believe it was untrue. No decent person wants to acknowledge the reality of that unspeakable sin. Now if you'll excuse me, I must go and prepare the child buggerer for burial. It has been a pleasure, marshal."

The marshal turned away with a disgusted sneer on his face. "Enchanting, sir, enchanting." Marshal Church continued on his way down the dusty street without another glance back.

At the end of the street he saw a corral filled with horses running around. He laid eyes on his own black stallion. On sighting him, Claudette began to slowly saunter over, willing to interrupt her play with the other horses, if only momentarily. The marshal walked up to the fence and clicked his tongue against his teeth. The horse responded immediately and trotted over, sticking her head over the fence and nuzzling his master.

"Oh girl, you won't be in here too long," the marshal said.

He reached into his pocket and pulled out a small handful of grain and fed it to the steed while he stroked her large black head and mane.

"You wouldn't be thinking 'bout stealing that nag and cutting town, would you?"

The accusatory voice came from the front steps of a home nearby. A man in an expensive suit stood on the porch and began to descend the short staircase. The marshal took a deep breath, let out an exasperated sigh, and turned to face the accusatory voice.

"No sir, I'm just making sure that my horse here is all fine and taken care of."

"Oh, she's taken care of all right," the man said. "And she is gonna stay there and be well taken care of until we find out who you really are, Mister Marshal. *If* that is indeed what you are."

The marshal looked at him and offered some false cordiality through squinting eyelids. "I don't believe I have ever made the acquaintance of someone in such a standoffish manner."

"Well, let me apologize sir," the man said sarcastically. "You have made the acquaintance of Carlyle George, local peddler of fine horse

The marshal extended his hand. The horse peddler hesitantly took it and gave it a quick shake but dropped it immediately. The marshal noticed and was offended by the man's lack of propriety.

"While I hesitate to say it's a pleasure to meet you sir, I am Marshal Church."

"Well, sure you are," said the man. "So, unless you're in the market for a house or a horse, I think you should probably mosey on and stay away from my pens."

"Now why would I wanna stick around and be interested in a house? I thought you wanted me to leave town, Mr. George."

"Hmm, oh well, you have to excuse me, that was just a habit, a figure of speech," said Carlyle. "I am the town's horse peddler as well as realtor in these parts. See, I represent a Mr. Allister Behan in our fine town here."

"The mayor. Yes, I've made his acquaintance," the marshal said with a sly grin.

"Yeah, our fine, upstanding mayor is also the primary landholder. He has invested his time and money through his honest business dealings. First as the town sheriff, then as the mayor, and he done purchased up these properties at a generous price from the townsfolk, and now rents out these fine homes and establishments to the fair folk of Burlton."

"Sounds like your mayor has an entire town under his thumb," the marshal remarked.

"Well, hold on with the accusations there, marshal. I'm sure you know as a man of the law that making accusations without evidence that's, that's akin to being a liar and we know people around here don't accuse people of being liars, except you."

The marshal gritted his teeth and looked at the man.

"Well, since I've been here, I do believe that heavier accusations of lies and identity have been leveled on myself from you and your kin and your friends. If you want to talk about making accusations without evidence, there is a man being displayed on the street down there with some horrible accusations leveled toward him, with apparently no evidence. Sounds like the only mistake he ever made was maybe challenging your fair mayor."

With that, Carlyle's face turned several shades of red. He huffed and glared at the marshal.

"I don't care if you're a man of the law or not," he said. "You need to stay out of the affairs of Burlton. You ain't one of us, you ain't from here, and you better keep your nose out of it. Move along as quickly as you can, stranger."

"Is that so? Is there anything else you advise me, sir?" The marshal responded evenly. Carlyle decided to change tack.

"I'm sorry, sir. I'm not looking for a confrontation with a lawman like yourself about this. How about if I just leave one of these doors unlocked and you can take your horse when no one's looking, and you can ride out of town. They might not have time to catch you and hunt you down before they figure out you're gone." The marshal looked at him, narrowing his eyes.

"Oh, I appreciate the offer, friend, but I think I'll stay here and I'll face my judgment."

"Let me know if you change your mind," said Carlyle.

"The only thing I would change my mind about," said the marshal, "is allowing my horse to stay in such a filthy, unkept pen, surrounded by nags who have been starved and beat and injured." Carlyle's face turned red again.

"Now sir, I have attempted to be civil with you, but you are leveling some very, very offensive accusations at me. These are all fine steeds and well taken care of, and I personally inspect everyone one of them and care for them very well."

"Define well," said the marshal. Carlyle looked at him silently, glaring for a moment.

"I do believe I'm finished with this conversation, sir." The marshal glared back at the horse peddler.

"Then why don't you move on back up to your porch leave me alone?"

"I'd be happy to, sir, I'll do just that, but in the meantime, you stay away from my horses. You stay away from that pen or someone might think you're trying to take off."

With that, Carlyle nervously backed up the porch steps, never taking his eyes off the marshal, and entered his home apparently deciding that he no longer needed the air or the sun out on the porch. The marshal took a quick look at the horses in the pen. He saw a feedbag tied shut, hanging on a post on the corner of the pen. He fished around in his gun belt holding only Cletus's colt six-shooter and flipped open the small pocket containing his hunting knife. He stabbed the knife into the bag and pulled it sideways, bisecting it, and spilled its guts of rolled oats into a heap on the ground. As the marshal turned and walked away back down the street, hungry horses scampered over and began gorging themselves on the feed. His own black steed stood silently watching her master walk away.

Feeling a twinge of vehemence deep in chest, the marshal turned his attention to the quiet, empty looking church. He walked up the front steps and opened the wide double doors. The pews were empty, the altar candles flickered, but apparently, nobody was around. The marshal walked up and looked at the giant 10-foot-tall statue of Jesus on the cross, carved out of oak and inlaid with immaculate adornments; a wreath of thorns around Jesus' head that appeared to be crafted from pure gold along with other trinkets and candleholders that seemed very lavish for the little town. He heard a murmur from a room in the back behind the altar. He ambled in, spurs on his boots clanking and echoing in the quiet church.

In the back room, a thin, gaunt man in a black and red robe kneeled over a nervous young boy crouched on a chair.

"I want to show you how the Lord manifests the pleasure of his divinity," the pastor whispered to the young boy.

"It is a fine day for God's work!" the marshal said loudly from the doorway. The pastor rolled his eyes in frustration and exhaled loudly.

"I am not currently taking confessions, sir. Please come back at a later time. I am busy training this young man for the service of the Lord."

"What service is that?" asked the marshal, his voice booming.

"He is an altar boy, and I am teaching him his duties as such," the pastor retorted.

"What part of being an altar boy involves having a lecherous old man bend over you in a chair, making him as scared as a little squirrel?" the marshal asked.

The pastor's eyes went wide and he stood abruptly and turned, about to release some form of fervent, godly range on an unsuspecting member of the town's folk. He stopped himself, realizing that he was facing the marshal he had heard so much about.

"Well, then." The man suddenly became meek, bending down and placing his hands together begging pardon. "I am sorry for my tone. You must be that marshal that I heard about in town."

"Again, it seems my reputation does proceed me, sir."

"Yes, yes, I've heard. I can tell. You look like a great marshal and I am sure that you will prove your identity. We will be happy to make your acquaintance and provide hospitality to you in our fair town. You are welcome to take confession right now."

Unimpressed, the marshal looked down at the man in the red and black robe. "I don't need to confess anything, sir. Least of all to you."

The pastor looked confused. "I'm sorry, sir, have I offended you in some way?"

The marshal glared at him. "No, but you have offended that boy with what unspeakable acts you were about to do to him."

The pastor now took offense. "I am sorry, sir, but I am a man of the Lord—"

"And that don't give you no right to commit an ungodly act." the marshal interrupted.

The pastor began to stammer incoherently and nervously. The marshal looked behind the man at the boy in the chair.

"You get out of here, son. Your work here for the Lord is done for the day. You don't come back here."

The boy nervously grabbed his stuff and left the room quickly. A faint "Thanks, mister," was heard as the boy scampered past the pews toward the exit. The pastor became angry again.

"How dare you come into this house of the Lord and level such horrible accusations!"

The marshal looked back at him, his face doing nothing to hide his anger. "I'll do more than level. So far nothing has happened, I simply wanted to come by and meet the townsfolk. I figured it would be a good idea to make the acquaintance of the local pastor."

"Well, you have not made a good impression," the pastor responded.

The marshal reached a hand out and looked the pastor in the eye. "Marshal Lloyd Church Jr., sir."

The pastor nervously extended a shaky hand. "Pastor Josiah Behan."

The marshal squinted his eyes. "And kin to your fine mayor and sheriff and the like here in Burlton, correct?" He didn't let go of the pastor's hand.

"Yes sir, proud, proud brother to both of those fine upstanding men."

"And how did you come to such a righteous path, Pastor?" the marshal asked.

"Well," the pastor explained, "I believe all of my brothers are doing the Lord's work and we all just chose different paths to do that work."

The pastor's hand began to sweat. The marshal looked at him skeptically.

"Well, if what you're all doing is the Lord's work, then the people of this fine town are in a lot of trouble."

With that, the marshal disgustedly released his grip on the pastor's hand and turned and walked out of the room. He stalked swiftly past the pews and behind him the disheveled pastor ran out of the back chamber, yelling at the marshal.

"You can't just come into the house of the Lord and treat it with such disrespect. You won't get away with it!"

As the marshal walked out of the door, he muttered, "I don't intend to."

Marshal Lloyd Church cooled his temper as he walked down the street. His steps were heavy; he wanted to vent the growing anger inside but suppressed it. He had managed to cool his head just enough to be civil by the time he found himself in front of the bordello He took a deep breath and entered. As he walked in the door, he saw women in all manner of dress and undress, flirting and laughing with men at various levels of intoxication. Some of the men were wearing deputy stars. Others were just associated with those men. There was a sudden crash next to the marshal's head. He quickly drew his pistol and looked around, preparing for a confrontation.

"How dare you come in here, you scum-sucking weasel!"

The voice came from across the room. A woman in a too-small black corset and bustier with disheveled hair came tromping over to him. She had thrown a glass of scotch at the marshal which had busted on the wall beside him.

"What kind of a greeting is that, ma'am?"

"The only greeting you'll get in these parts," said the madam. "This here is my establishment and I don't welcome your kind here."

"I do believe we have not met, ma'am, so I'm not sure what I have done to offend you." The marshal observed, replacing his gun in its holster.

"You have offended my family and my family's honor," she said. "I am Drusilla Behan, owner of this here cathouse and you have vexed many of my kinfolk in the short time you have been here."

The marshal took a deep breath and removed his hat.

"I do apologize for any perceived disrespect, ma'am. I did not come here for any kind of confrontation."

"So then, what are you doing here?" she asked brusquely.

"Well, ma'am, I was hoping for some time with one of your ladies."

The marshal reached inside his jacket and pulled out his coin sack. It was filled with coins similar to the one he had given Sam the night before and the woman at the diner that morning. Drusilla's attitude quickly changed. A smile slowly spread across her face. She gave the marshal a knowing grin.

"Well, I guess even a man of the law does need to have his needs met, doesn't he?" she crowed. "I'm willing to overlook the slight against my family for the time being." She took the sack of money the marshal offered and tucked it into her brassiere. She gave him a seductive look up and down. "Well, now, you're welcome to any one of my fine ladies."

She turned and gestured to a group of women in their undergarments sitting on stools along the wall. "I might even be able to carve out some time myself for you if you'd like, mister marshal," she said breathily.

The marshal looked up and down at Drusilla's aging, frumpy frame. "I do very much appreciate that offer, Miss Behan . . ."

The marshal looked up at a slim female figure in a bustier whose fine, light blonde hair was curled up on top of her head and was gazing down on the proceedings over a railing from the upstairs loft. She had beautiful, porcelain doll-type features; a small nose, a pointed chin, and bright red lipstick. She had an elegant, powder blue dress over her undergarments.

"But I would like to spend my time with her," the marshal said, smiling.

Moments later, the marshal and the young woman he had chosen were alone in her chamber. The marshal closed the door and nervously placed his hat on the coat hanger. He turned to face the woman, who a moment ago had been sitting on the bed. He was startled to see that she had risen and was standing right in front of him. She gave him a quick and stinging slap. He held his jaw, rubbing the sting away and looked back at her.

"And what was that for?" the marshal asked.

"I know who you are," the woman said angrily.

"I still don't know what I did to deserve that, miss," he responded.

"You . . . how dare you come back here? You abandoned me!"

"I was doing what I had to do," the marshal said quietly.

"What you 'had to do'? You could've stayed here; you could've protected me! Now, look at you."

"Look at me? Look at you!" the marshal blurted in exasperation. "What are you doing here, Nancy? What are you doing to yourself? You weren't meant for this! You had a respectable family. You were never meant to give yourself away to men for money."

"Yeah, well, we didn't have very many options, did we?" Nancy DeLacey responded crossly. "Once my parents were gone and the Behan's took over their business, what else was I going to do? I didn't have anyone to support me. I had to support myself."

"What happened to your brother?" Lloyd asked with concern.

"He accused one of Behan's deputies of cheating at cards . . . they shot him dead before he got his gun out of his holster."

A somber look of regret passed over the marshal's face. "I could've supported you."

"How were you going to do that?" Nancy questioned, "when you were gone for five years?"

"Five years? You could've come with me, Nancy."

"You knew I couldn't. My parents were dead and it was all we could do to keep the business running. Now the Behan's run the mill and the bank like it's their own personal Fort Knox."

"The Behan's?" the marshal questioned in surprise. "The Behan's . . ."

"Yeah, the Behan's. The ones who run this town, and if you want to live to see sunrise tomorrow, you best stop riling them up."

"Listen, I came back, I'm here to fix things. I'm here to save you."

"I don't want your saving!" Nancy yelled. "You've already abandoned me, you don't get to come back and *un*abandon me. I've made my choices and I've survived on my own. You're not welcome here."

The marshal hung his head in shame. "I really wanted to see you again, Nancy. I think about you all the time."

"Well, that's too bad, because I don't think about you anymore. At all." She sat back down on the bed, crossed her arms, and looked at the marshal. "Are you still expecting the time you paid for?"

The marshal turned and took his hat off the hook. "No, Nancy, I just wanted to see you, that's all."

"Well, now you've seen me," Nancy responded curtly.

"I'm sorry miss," the marshal replied. "Thank you for your time."

He turned and left the room. Without a word or making eye contact with anyone else, he quickly stomped down the stairs and out the front door of the brothel. Drusilla Behan grinned watching the man leave.

"Hell, I could've squeezed in a couple minutes for him," Drusilla laughed. Of course, her laughter was joined by other whores and lecherous whoremongers in the room.

The marshal wandered through the street without any direction in mind, trying to walk off his frustrations. By now he'd had a very eventful day of introductions and feather-ruffling in the town of Burlton. He was wandering toward Sam's saloon when a whistle caught his attention. A waving hand in the air beckoned him over. It was the doctor and druggist, McCoolie, standing in front of his dispensary accompanied by the sheriff.

"Good news, marshal!" McCoolie shouted, smiling. The marshal walked over to him. "Whoa boy, that is the fastest response I have ever gotten from a telegraph," McCoolie exclaimed. "You must know some high up folks up there in Washington."

"I told you, I'm a Federal Marshal representing the president himself."

"That you are, that you are," the sheriff said. "We got confirmation this afternoon, sir, we apologize for the inconvenience. We will be happy to return your belongings and let you be getting on your way to go do that honorable work for our fine president."

"That's great, thank you, I'm just going to go back to Sam's and gather up my belongs. I would like to issue a thank you to the entire community for the hospitality they have shown me. If you could do me a favor and get all your people and all your family, and all your fine folks together. Just, you know, spread the word, let people know that I'd like to personally thank the fine citizens of Burlton for all of the warmth they've shown me since I've been here."

The sheriff looked at him a little puzzled. "Well sir, on account of the fact that you are a Federal Marshal, I think we'll be happy to oblige, and we will do that sir, thank you, marshal."

"Let's say an hour in front of the sheriff's station?"

"An hour then . . . six o'clock," the sheriff said. "Right after dinner."

"Much obliged," the marshal nodded.

Marshal Church then turned and walked back to Sam's. The marshal pushed open the door and ignored the wave of hushes and whispers that he had become accustomed to in this town. He ignored the drunks and the deputies falling over themselves inebriated. He walked up to the bar and slapped his hand on the counter.

"Whiskey, Sam." Sam looked at him.

"Looks like you got something wearing on you, marshal," Sam said The marshal took the shot glass full of whiskey and poured it down his throat, then slammed the glass back down on the bar. As Sam refilled it the marshal looked at him.

"I think you all have something wearing on you around these parts," said the marshal seriously. He slugged back the next shot and placed the glass back down. Sam looked at him a little hesitantly.

"Is that so, marshal?"

The marshal downed another shot.

"Yeah, I believe that's so," he replied. Marshal Church slammed the shot glass back on the counter.

"What do you intend to do about it?" Sam asked hesitantly, filling the glass yet again. The marshal slammed back another shot.

"I intend to right some wrongs, Sam, and make it so that you don't have to pay insurance to protect your place."

Sam stopped and put his hand over the full shot glass, preventing the surprised marshal from taking another shot. The marshal looked up at him in disbelief.

"If you plan on doing all that, you don't need more of this," Sam said, quite matter-of-factly. "What you need is in back here behind the bar."

An hour later the sheriff and his deputies, all mostly piss-drunk, were in front of the sheriff's station. The marshal approached the sheriff's station. True to his word, the sheriff had assembled his men and the marshal's belongings on the front porch of the station. Many of the townswhat the marshal had to say and merrily send him off. The marshal stood in front of the sheriff's station and spoke to all the members of the community that had gathered.

"People of Burlton," he began. "I did tell your sheriff that I wanted to assemble all of you so you could personally hear my thanks for your hospitality . . . or for what passes as hospitality in your community." A gasp went up through the astonished crowd.

"As they have confirmed, my name is Lloyd Church Jr., duly appointed Federal Marshal representing the president himself. I have been held up here in Burlton while they confirmed my identity, being as I was a stranger entering your town, and they had believed that I had maybe slighted your fine lawmen here. Now these things are confirmed and my belongings are back with me and now your fine lawman is happy to see me head on out of town," he paused and turned to look at the sheriff. "Isn't that, right?"

The sheriff nodded and said, "God be with you." A chuckle erupted through the lawmen and kinfolk hanging about.

"Well, I appreciate that, sheriff. I appreciate every fine, law-abiding, upstanding citizen of this town, and I do believe that they will appreciate my words. As I told you, I am a Federal Marshal representing the President of the United States, and I have upon me 30 warrants and bounties sworn out. I have been charged with the task to enforce them on some of the most wanted men in America. I do apologize for a slight deception on my part—"

The sheriff interrupted. "And we are happy to have been here to show you our hospitality, or as you say, 'what passes for hospitality', and now you can go off and do your work."

The marshal chuckled. "Well thank you, sheriff. As I said, I do apologize for any deception on my part. You see, I already am doing my work." He looked at the lawmen on the porch in front of him in all their glory; tin stars, dirty hats, and smug sneers on their faces. "I am here to arrest you all."

Chapter Six

Audible gasps rippled through the gathered crowd. Anxious, uneasy expressions spread across the lawmen's faces as they looked back and forth at each other.

"Well, that doesn't make no sense. What y'all mean by that, Mr. Marshal?"

Cletus sat atop the marshal's saddle as it straddled the railing of the porch. The rat-faced deputy held his gas lantern aloft in the early evening dusk, shooting a suspicious look at Marshal Church.

"Well, folks, let me tell you a story," the marshal replied. "About fifteen years ago, one of the most wanted gangs in the United States rode into town. The Shannon gang was a family of criminals and their associates who had terrorized and robbed citizens across the country. They were wanted on several counts of rape, murder, horse wrangling, and thievery in Utah, Idaho, and several other regions of the Union. They came into this fair town and decided that they had a new plan.

"They didn't want to run and they didn't want to go to Mexico. Instead, they murdered the sheriff and his family and left his son to die in a burning house. The boy escaped crawled into the dirt and cried himself to sleep. The next morning, he sifted through the ashes of his home and found the remnants of his father's ammunitions. He loaded three unspent shells into a burnt old six-shooter. He walked into town, and wiped the tears from his face."

WHEN I GOT THERE, I saw some of these strangers. I recognized their voices from the night before when they killed my family, so I knew who they were. My pa had told me they were the Shannon gang and I heard them talking to the townsfolk. One of them held a Bible and wore spectacles as he talked to the pastor.

"We witnessed it. We saw the house aflame and we are very sorry to hear what must've happened to your sheriff. As a fellow man of God, I am truly appalled by what has transpired," said the thin one.

"We just wanted to ride into your town and find out if bandits had done to you what they did out there." said another man on a horse.

I recognized his voice as being the leader of the Shannon gang. I slowly crept up; no one took notice of a dirty ten-year-old boy with shaky hands who was nervously leveling a pistol. Some of the townsfolk had begun to gather, but still, no one took notice of me. I crept right up and pointed that gun; I was ready. My hands were unsteady but I was close enough.

Suddenly, a hand reached down, knocked the gun from my grasp, and grabbed my wrist. I looked up. It was a dignified-looking man in a bowler hat who was finely dressed, especially compared to the soot-covered rags I was in. He gave me a severe, warning look. The commotion caught the attention of the newcomers to town. Before any of the regular townsfolk could get a very good look at me, the man with the Bible spoke.

"Aw, now. Look at you, little urchin. Looks like a homeless child. As God is my witness, I think we will take you in and teach you the ways of the Lord." The man grinned at me with a greasiness that made me squirm.

The gentleman who had slapped the gun out of my hand, which now resided unseen between the feet of his horse, stepped forward. He looked at the self-described man of God and noticed how the man had looked at me and licked his lips. My unexpected protector spoke up.

"I do believe you are mistaken," he said in a British accent. "This here is my boy."

The churchgoer looked up in astonishment at the British gentleman.

"Well now, pardon me for my surprise. It just seems that you are so much more elegantly dressed than this young man. I did not believe that you were acquainted."

"I do apologize," the British man said pleasantly. "My youngster came out here in such a rush when he heard you had arrived that he did not take the time to get properly dressed as is expected of him." He gently placed a hand on my shoulder.

"Is that so?" the churchgoer asked me. "Is that right, boy? Is this here your daddy?"

The British man peered down at me sternly with the same warning in his eyes. I looked back at the man and lied.

"Yes'm, sir," I said.

"Well, isn't that funny?" remarked the churchgoer suspiciously. "He sure don't sound like you, Mr. British Gentleman."

"Well," the man responded, "he takes after his mother."

A few minutes later the man hustled me away from the gathering townsfolk, jumped on his horse, and began to trot out of town.

"What did you do that for?" I asked as I walked alongside the horse he was riding.

"Because you weren't going to do anything but get yourself into a whole big mess of trouble."

"Those men killed my family. My daddy—"

"I know who your daddy is," the man interrupted, "and he was a fine man and I'm sorry for your loss. I genuinely am, but you getting your young self killed by playing around with guns and bandits is not going to help serve their memory at all."

"But they're outlaws and I need to get revenge," I said irritably.

"No. What you need to do," the British man said authoritatively, "is to get away from here. You're a little boy. Those are grown men who do nothing but kill and steal. Going around and playing with guns won't do you any good."

"Where are we going, mister?" I asked, since we were leaving the town behind.

"We're heading to my home and I'm going to get you a hot lunch and we'll figure things out from there."

"Well, how far is it, then?"

"Just about nine more miles."

"How come you live so far outside of town?" I asked inquisitively.

"Well, son, let's just say I am happy to serve the fine folk of Burlton, but I also very much like to keep myself and keep my business, *my* business. I enjoy the privacy afforded me by living a fair distance away, out in the desert."

> "Well, if it's so far, mister, if you don't mind, you think
> I could get up on the horse, too?" The British gentleman
> chuckled, "I apologize."

He helped hoist me up into the saddle. I clung to him as we rode miles to his home. My finger gently brushed the burnt pistol I had picked up after the incident in front of the church.

We arrived at the gentleman's home. It was simple; just three rooms, but very, very neat and nicely decorated. It looked like the kind of fine British homes I had read about in some of my chap books.

After about 20 minutes of awkward silence, got out two bowls, placed them on the table and uncovered a pot of something aromatic on the stove.

"So, what are we going to do now?" I asked hesitantly.

"Well, I don't know," said the gentleman, "but I suppose I'm going to take care of you, if you want me to."

"What makes you think I can't take care of myself?" I asked, confident in my imagined independence.

"Well," the gentleman said, "because you're a ten-year-old boy and you always had your family around to help you out, and now you don't . . ."

I looked solemnly at the floor as he scooped something from the pot into the bowls, then continued kindly, "And chasing those bandits isn't going to do anything to help honor the memory of your family. So, if it's okay with you I'm going to take care of you and we're going to keep you from being found by the rest of those bandits."

"How are we going to do that, though?" I asked anxiously. "What about church and going to school? They're sure to see me. Someone's eventually bound to tell them I'm here."

"Well, that's a good point," the gentleman said. "Here's what we'll do: I'll educate you here at home when I'm not busy with my clothing store. You help maintain things around here. You keep an eye on the chickens and the pigs and help with that, since it's more than I can handle myself anyway. When I'm not busy with the store, I'll school you in the most important things." He pointed to a chair and I sat.

"What're the most important things, mister? Are you able to teach me the same stuff I've been learning in school?" I took a look at the strange looking stuff in my bowl.

"Well, maybe not the same things, not exactly." said the gentleman, "but I can tell you what's important, and that's how to be a gentleman. So, why don't you eat up and we'll have our first lesson?"

Later, the British gentleman looked at me and my stomach full of a spicy dish he told me was called curry. It was very different than anything my ma had ever made, and I wasn't sure if I really cared for the spices, but I couldn't argue with a full belly.

"Lesson number one," the British man said, "a gentleman never lets a door slam in someone's face. Now let's try it. You're walking ahead of me and we are going through the door, simple as that."

We went outside and I walked in like I always did, my hand pressing the door backward behind me as I entered. The door slammed right in the gentleman's face. I laughed. He opened the door and looked at me.

"What was that?"

I couldn't help but giggle at the ridiculous situation.

"I'm sorry," I said, "Ma just always told me to close the door behind me, it's a habit."

I tried not to think of my ma right then. The memory of my love for her and what the Shannon gang did to her was still too raw and painful.

The gentleman chuckled. "That's all right. It's perfectly fine to do that when you're by yourself, but you want to make sure that you hold the door for somebody if they are coming in behind you. Then gently close the door behind them, that way you avoid closing the door in somebody's face."

"All right, if you say so, sir," I said. "Why is that so important? How does this door matter at all?"

"Son, this is part of being a gentleman."

"Why is being a gentleman so important?"

My new benefactor looked at me earnestly. "Because son, the only thing that is going to save common decent folk is being kind and decent to each other. The best way that you can live is to be an example, not end up like those men that took your family from you. If we all would act more like gentlemen, then our lives would be a whole lot better, don't you think?"

"I guess you're right then, sir," I said, uncertainly. "I just don't see why the door's that important."

"The door is just one thing," said the British gentleman, "there's a lot more to learn about being a gentleman and being civilized, but let's work on this first."

Over the following weeks I helped to make sure the chicken and the pigs were fed while the gentleman was selling clothes from his store in town. In the evenings, I would help him slaughter an animal if we needed it for food, and he would teach me about being a gentleman. Mr. Aberdeen taught me things like: facial hair is temporary, but tattoos are permanent; he taught me to know when to say nothing; and even if I felt like I was more well-educated than someone else I would not hold it in their face. He called that 'wearing your learning lightly'. He brought me some clothes in my size and explained that every gentleman must have one well-made dark suit, one tweed suit, and a dinner jacket. He taught me to polish my shoes and to say my name when being introduced.

One day after several weeks in the British gentleman's care, shortly after he had gotten home from the clothing shop, I heard the thunder of hooves approaching the house. I panicked, scrambled to the cot in the corner of the living room that the gentleman had set up for me, and fumbled to find the pistol I had hidden. I was terrified. All I could think of was the sound of those hooves that approached my home before my family was killed. I went outside and saw one lone man heading toward the house at full speed. I couldn't make out who he was; I didn't recognize him. I was frightened and my hands shook but I lifted that iron as the man approached.

I yelled out, "You, stop!"

He was a thin man with a big orange mustache and a white cowboy hat. He wore a shirt with some medals pinned to the shoulder, but I didn't much care about what kind of medals he had or what they looked like. I just knew he was a stranger heading toward me and I was fixing to protect myself.

He stopped and stared at me. "What is going on here?" he asked loudly in a thick Southern accent.

Mr. Aberdeen came out and peeked around the corner, startled by the sight of me holding a gun. He stumbled over, stammering crossly.

"What—what are you doing? I do not allow guns in this house. Keep that thing pointed down." He came out and for the second time since I met the man, he forced the gun from my hand, this time taking it and tucking it in his waistband. "That is not the way a gentleman greets a stranger," he scolded me. He turned and he looked at the stranger on the horse in front of us.

"Matthew?" he asked, puzzled. The man just smiled at him. "Oh my God, Matthew!" The man dismounted his pale horse and took the lead.

"Imagine my surprise to find a young man armed outside your home," the stranger said.

"Who is this fellow, then?" I asked.

The two men laughed and slapped each other on the shoulders as if they were the best of friends. Mr. Aberdeen hugged him in greeting, a grin spreading ear to ear. He looked the happiest I'd ever seen him.

"Young Lloyd, this is my very dear friend, Matthew Sanders. I didn't expect you, Matthew! I apologize, I'm not prepared."

"No need," Matthew responded.

"You don't need to get prepared, anymore." He looked at my benefactor with a sly twinkle in his eye.

"What do you mean, Matthew?" the gentleman questioned.

"I am now officially retired from the United States Cavalry. I'm free to do with my time as I please."

The British gentleman laughed and hugged his friend. They slapped each other's shoulders some more. And even though I thought that the gentleman could not have looked any happier, he did. He was so happy I thought he was going to cry.

"Come on in, then, come on in."

The two men walked inside the house and I followed curiously. The gentleman finished preparing a pork dinner that he had started before Matthew arrived.

"So, what are you doing here, then?" I asked the stranger. "And who are you?"

"Well, as Mr. Aberdeen here explained to you, son, my name is Matthew Sanders. I'm a retired member of the U.S. Cavalry and veteran of the War of Northern Aggression."

Mr. Aberdeen laughed over his shoulder and said with a smile.

"Nobody calls it that, Matthew. It's called the 'Civil War.'"

"There was nothing civil about it as far as I saw." Matthew said in his Southern drawl. "But I was in it, and now I'm retired."

"So, you were on the side of the South in the Civil War?" I asked the man with the bushy, mustache.

"Yes, I was, son."

"What are you doing here? Why did you ever do that? You must be right mad that we don't have slaves anymore."

"Well son, that is a complicated issue, you see, I never really thought we should have had slaves in the first place."

"But you fought for the South! Why did you fight for the South if you didn't agree with them?"

Mr. Sanders looked at me seriously, his tone had changed and the look on Mr. Aberdeen's face had also become more solemn as he dished out dinner for us.

"Well son, you see, I was on the side of the South because I am from the South and that was the only side to be on."

"But did you have to go to war to fight for something you didn't believe in?"

"Well, it wasn't just that son. You see, my daddy had always been disappointed in me; he thought I was weak. As I got older he grew more and more upset with me. There was an incident with a young fellow at school and he decided that he was going to disown me. He said he would no longer recognize me as his son. So, in my infinite young wisdom, I decided that if I was to enlist for the South that I would earn back my daddy's respect."

"Did it work, mister?"

"No. Some things, some people just can't accept. I eventually learned how pointless it was to try to win my dad's acceptance and respect. I just had to have respect for myself. And although I never got what I wanted from him, I had already enlisted myself and obligated myself to this great nation. I traveled and I did many, many, many deeds on behalf of our new union. Once the South ceded I knew I was safe to represent the beliefs I believed in, and I believed that someday our country would be able to accept all kinds of people."

"What do you mean, sir?" I asked. "Don't we believe in that now? Aren't we free and united?"

Mr. Aberdeen gave me a sideways look, and patted Matthew on the shoulder as he passed him a steaming bowl.

"Well son, that's the idea but we still got a lot of work to do . . . We still got a lot of work to do."

As we sat at the table, Matthew blew at the steam coming from his bowl. I followed suit mimicking him. Mr. Aberdeen looked up at both of us and then at me, chuckling.

"Lloyd, Mr. Sanders is going to stay here with us for a while, would that be all right with you?"

I looked at Mr. Aberdeen and then at Mr. Sanders.

"Yeah, I think that will be all right."

The two men looked at each other and grinned. We made a quick meal of our pork stew.

THE FOLLOWING DAY WAS one of the best days I'd had since I'd gone to live at Mr. Aberdeen's. That was because while Mr. Aberdeen was busy at the store, Matthew was there to help me out with the chores and keeping the livestock. While it used to take me all day to get things done, we had finished by early afternoon so we found ourselves with some free time. I went through Mr. Aberdeen's books and was trying to find something I'd be interested in reading when Matthew approached me.

"So, you want to be a hotshot with the iron, boy?"

I looked up at him. "What do you mean?"

"Well, since you drew that pistol on me yesterday, I assume you must be a real crack shot."

"Well, not really," I said. "My pa, he was a sheriff and I want to be just like him. I wanted to be a sheriff, too. But now Mr. Aberdeen says the best thing I can do is just be a gentleman."

"Well son, there are advantages to being a gentleman but there are also advantages to being able to defend yourself."

"Are you a gentleman?" I asked Mr. Sanders.

"Yes sir, but I'm a little bit of a different type of gentleman. I live by what is called the code of honor, something we use in the South. Very much like Mr. Aberdeen's British gentleman's code of conduct, but we also know how to protect our own. Here, I want you to gather up these cans and some of these old looking books, the ones that he doesn't seem to read anymore, and I want you to bring them out back to the fence over the pigpen."

I did as Mr. Sanders instructed and when I got out there I found him waiting. We took the gathered items and lined them up on top of the fence.

Then he said, "Follow me, boy." We walked about a dozen yards before he turned to me. "Are you ready?"

"Sure enough, I guess," I said. He then slipped his hand into his gun belt, took a pistol from the holster and handed it to me.

"You're going to point and you're going to shoot, that's what we're going to work on right now; pointing and shooting." My hands shook but Mr. Sanders spoke to me serenely. "All right now, first what you have to do is breathe deeply," he said. "Relax, be calm. You're not in trouble, you're just pointing the gun at a can. Now I want you to take a deep breath and—"

Bang!

The gun went off before Mr. Sanders finished his sentence. The sound of a bullet flying rang into the desert. I rubbed my ears.

"All right then," Mr. Sanders said. "Now we're going to take that one step slower. I'm just going to take the bullets out of this gun." He took the pistol from my hand and emptied the remaining five cartridges.

"Now, we're just going to breathe deeply, and make sure that we have that barrel sighted at what we wanna shoot at first." Knowing the gun wasn't loaded, I calmed down very quickly. I aimed the gun at one of the cans on the fence.

"Now breathe deep, and what you want to do is slowly squeeze the trigger. You don't need to jerk it, you don't need to pull it fast, just squeeze the trigger." Matthew instructed.

I relaxed and pointed the gun at the can, slowly pulled the trigger, and heard the gun click.

"All right, that's great. Now what we're going to do, we're going to practice that a few times, okay? When I think you have that part down, we're going to add to it."

"Okay, Mr. Sanders," I said, encouraged.

I quickly started pointing at objects on the fence and pulled the trigger and clicked the gun.

"No, no, no, son, you're getting carried away," he said. "The same thing we did before; you have to know in your heart and your head that the gun is loaded and dangerous even when it's not, do you understand me? You have to slow down, you have to breathe, you got to squeeze the trigger every time you point that thing, and you don't point it unless you intend to use it, okay?" I understood the seriousness in Mr. Sander's voice.

"Okay," I said.

He stood and watched me as I slowly pointed at each object on the fence, inhaled and exhaled calmly, then clicked the gun in a steady, successive pace. I eyed up each object several times, firing imaginary bullets at them. This went on for about twenty minutes.

"Okay, now we're going to add cocking the hammer, which means you're going to lift your thumb and you're going to pull this hammer back until it clicks and it stays in place, okay? Now this hammer is what hits the cap in your ammunition, which will then launch a bullet from the gun. If you don't cock this hammer, it will not ignite the cap and it will not fire the bullet."

"Okay, sir," I said. "Are we going to add the bullets again, now?"

"Not at all," said Mr. Sanders, "not at all."

MR. ABERDEEN CONTINUED to train me in the ways of being a gentleman. During the day Mr. Sanders taught me about the Southern code of honor and how to fire a gun, and in the evenings Mr. Aberdeen explained to me how to be a gentleman and how to conduct myself in civilized society. They both emphasized that if I ever wanted to get revenge for what had happened to my family, I would need to use the law and retaliate in a civilized manner.

I had been firing bullets in the gun for about a week and was getting really good when Mr. Sanders started to show me some trick shots. He placed several objects all over the roof of the pigpen and the fence.

"Anyone can just shoot a man with a gun," he said. "It takes a real gunfighter, a real marksman, to shoot him without hurting him, to disarm another man without killing him."

"Are you a marksman?" I asked Mr. Sanders.

He grinned at me while he walked back to the pigpen. "You tell me, son." With that, he turned like a bolt of lightning and drew both guns before I saw them even come out of their holsters. He fired seven bullets that somehow managed to take out ten objects: an empty molasses can off the roof of the pigpen, a book off one of the fence posts, a whole series of cans, and even the egg whisk that he had pulled out of the kitchen that Mr. Aberdeen used regularly for cooking.

MATTHEW SHOT THE LIGHTS out, literally. One afternoon he assembled some old gas lanterns up that had outlived their usefulness, the glass domes obscured with soot and age. He pulled off a trick where he fired a bullet at a cast iron door from the old wood stove outside and it ricocheted off and took out a lamp that he had placed on the roof of the pig shed. I was still practicing, trying to get more than one object with one bullet in a straight line. One of those afternoons when I was eying up a bullet, eying out a shot with three cans lined up on top of the fence rail, I aimed, exhaled slowly, and pulled the trigger

"*BLAAM!*"

The bullet fired through all three cans and they toppled off the fence.

"Phew!" I sighed.

I smiled to myself and held the smoking pistol toward the sky proudly. I turned and not ten yards behind me I saw Mr. Aberdeen on his horse, home early from his clothing store, looking at me harshly.

"What the hell do you think you're doing?" Mr. Aberdeen demanded.

"I just . . . Matthew has been showing me how to—" He held his hand up, signaling me to be silent.

"Matthew has been showing you?" Mr. Aberdeen dismounted Claudia, a beautiful black mare that he rode every day to and from the clothing store.

He briskly walked to the door of the house and he yelled for Matthew to come outside.

"Matthew, we need to talk!"

Matthew came to the door a little bit puzzled. "What's got in your bonnet?" Mathew queried. He walked out shielding his eyes from the sunlight.

"Why is he outside shooting a gun?" Mr. Aberdeen asked crossly.

"Gerald, I know how you feel about this—" Matthew started before he was interrupted.

"Yes, you do know how I feel about this. So why is he outside shooting a gun, and un-supervised?" Mr. Aberdeen's face began to take on a shade of red I hadn't seen before. I tried to intervene.

"Listen, Mr. Aberdeen, Matthew didn't mean any harm. He knows you don't like guns, but I needed to learn."

"You stop talking," said Mr. Aberdeen, "you don't know better right now, but he does. Matthew, you know that I don't allow guns in the house."

"Gerald, he's got to learn some time—"

"No, he doesn't!" Mr. Aberdeen interjected. "Carrying guns brings nothing but trouble! Carrying a gun means that it's more likely that you're going to do something horrible with it by making bad decisions, or you are going to end up killed by one—"

Now, it was Matthew's turn to interrupt.

"That may very well be, Gerald, but he needs to at least learn how to use one, how to handle one, how to protect himself. What happens next time? What happens when bandits come to our home?"

"Don't give me that," said Mr. Aberdeen who then looked at me. "Don't fall into the trap of fearing the world because some bad things happen."

Matthew spoke out, "Yeah, and look at what happened to him!" He gestured to me. "Look at what happened to his family, look what's happened to each of us. We've all seen bad things happen, we've all had horrible things happen to us because of guns, but what would occur if we didn't have them to protect us when we needed them? I'm not saying that I want the kid to carry around six-shooters and walk through town firing them off at everyone that gives him a dirty eye, I'm saying that I am teaching the boy how to protect himself if he needs to."

Mr. Aberdeen said. "No, this is my home."

"*Your* home?" Matthew asked, offended. Mr. Aberdeen softened for a second and then his resolve returned.

"You know what I mean; I don't allow guns in this house."

"But Matthew always has his guns," I said, trying to justify the lessons. Mr. Aberdeen stared at me for a moment and then looked back at Mathew.

"Yes, he does, and from now on his guns are going to be mounted above the door where he can get them if he needs them, but they are going to stay there otherwise."

Matthew looked slightly aggravated at his British friend.

"Gerald, you know he needs to learn how to do this. He needs to be able to defend himself." Mr. Aberdeen looked back and forth at us and sternly.

"The guns will be mounted above the door where he can't get to them, but you can. They are only to be taken down to help young Lloyd learn how to shoot, or in the case of an emergency, and that is final." Mr. Aberdeen stomped away and gave the strap attached to Claudia's leather bridal a tug to take her back to the shed.

I looked up at Matthew. "I'm sorry, I didn't mean to—"

Matthew interrupted with a kind voice. "It's okay, you don't need to apologize. Some things are just a sore spot, you didn't do anything wrong."

So that night Matthew climbed up on the step stool and hammered four nails into the wall above the front door. On them he placed the six-shooters, each one hanging on two nails; one in front of the trigger and the other in front of the handle. Each pistol rested above the entrance to our home where they could be seen and taken down if needed. Matthew always made sure I was supervised when handling the guns and we never spoke of it again with Mr. Aberdeen.

Since Mr. Sanders and I had become so efficient with the chores, we often had free time in the afternoon. Mr. Sanders would read or tell me stories about his experiences in the Civil War. Every now and then I'd wander over to the River Glen and would sit by the cool waters getting my toes wet, and sometimes, climb in.

Since everyone in town thought I was dead, it was a very lonely existence. I often yearned to again see friends that I had in town, but Mr. Aberdeen continually told me it was much safer if we kept the fact that he was now taking care of me a secret. One of those afternoons, when I was about fourteen, I lingered a little longer by the river than I should have. The sun was going down, and I was going to be late for dinner. I knew that Mr. Aberdeen would beat me home but still I moseyed along and dawdled on my way, not too concerned because I knew Mr. Aberdeen would save me some vittles.

As I approached the door of the house I heard strange noises. Moaning and groaning come from inside. I peeked through the windows and I saw Matthew leaning over the kitchen table looking as if he was trying to jam something forcefully, like when he had a hard time getting a shoe on or off Claudia, or his pale horse, Dusty. Not thinking much of it, I went to the front door and slowly pushed it open. Everything was silent; even the door didn't make its usual squeak when it opened.

There, leaning over the kitchen table, I saw Mr. Aberdeen bent over. His eyes were closed and his face was turned toward me, grimacing in pain. His hands were over his head, gripping the sides of the table. Behind him, Matthew, with bare buttocks exposed, held on to Mr. Aberdeen's waist. There was an equally pained look on his face, and with closed eyes he was forcefully thrusting behind Mr. Aberdeen. They both made strange moans and grunts and I was sure that Matthew was hurting Mr. Aberdeen badly.

I was shocked into silence. My mind flashed back to that night when my family was killed and those men had had their way with my sister on the bed right above my head. I couldn't believe that Matthew was hurting Mr. Aberdeen in that way. I pulled the stool over and quietly reached up and grabbed a pistol from above the door. The pistol trembled in my nervous hands as I shook and slowly levelled it at Matthew.

"Stop it, you get off him!" I finally mustered the courage to shout. Both men suddenly stopped moving and looked stunned; Matthew scrambled to pull his pants up and fasten them. Mr. Aberdeen jostled sideways, half rolling off the table and knocked over a cup of lard that had deep finger grooves in the soft white substance.

"Now, hold on just a minute," said Mr. Aberdeen. "You point that gun somewhere else."

"Boy, you are going to get yourself into a lot of trouble!" Matthew said angrily.

"No, I'm not. What were you doing? Why are you telling me to put the gun down, Mr. Aberdeen? I can't believe you, Matthew! You've been waiting all this time just to hurt Mr. Aberdeen like that!"

"It's not what it looks like, son," said Matthew. "Now, put that gun down."

Confused, my hands wavered a little bit and I looked back and forth between the two men. "What do you mean?" I demanded.

Mr. Aberdeen held his hands out, palms down, and decided to reason with me.

"Lloyd, I know what it looks like, but it's not the same thing that happened to your sister, all right? What you saw was something that happens sometimes. You know how your mommy and daddy were in love?" Mr. Aberdeen spoke to me in a low, calm voice.

"Yes," I said, confused. My hands were still wavering; I wasn't sure what to think.

"Well, occasionally two people that are not a man and a woman fall in love. Sometimes, they are two men and they fall in love the same way."

"That's not normal," I replied quickly, repulsed. "The preacher said that's a sin."

"Well, the preacher has his own issues and I don't believe that God would hate any two people in love," said Mr. Aberdeen.

I thought for a moment. I was nervous and made no effort to hide my disgust.

"But you said you love me and that's why you take care of me. Does that mean that you want to do that to me?" I was horrified.

The tender look on Mr. Aberdeen's face suddenly fell as if his heart had dropped to his knees and he now felt as empty as he looked. I could tell my words had deeply hurt him, but I didn't know why.

Matthew's response was more aggressive. His face turned red and he gritted his teeth. Stepping forward he grabbed my hand and ripped the pistol out of it, then slapped me hard across the face.

"How dare you, boy?" he bellowed.

The unloaded pistol rattled on the floor. I looked up at Matthew, equally as hurt and shocked as Mr. Aberdeen had been. I began to struggle, loosened Matthew's grip on my wrist and pushed him away. I flung the door open and ran out to the barn.

I hopped on Clyde, the yearling mule Mr. Aberdeen had brought home for me a couple of months earlier, and took off into the desert. Mr. Aberdeen and Matthew both looked at each other anxiously and Mr. Aberdeen scrambled to the front door.

"Lloyd, come back, boy! We need to talk!"

I ignored him and kept going as his voice slowly faded into a distant echo. I wiped hot tears from my face with the sleeve of my shirt. I didn't know at the time, but Mr. Aberdeen and Matthew nervously awaited my return with a posse from town. I rushed to the only place that I remembered the exact location of; the home of Nancy DeLacey, my friend from Sunday school.

I knocked on Nancy's door, and when her family saw me they acted like they had seen a ghost. They were all shocked and stupefied to see me alive, but recovered quick enough and invited me in for a bowl of stew. Nancy cried and hugged me. She had developed into a lovely teenager, her golden hair flowing over her delicate features. They asked me where I'd been for the last few years and I told them the entire story. I told Nancy's parents how the Shannon's had come into our home and how I had tried to get revenge and then I was stopped by Mr. Aberdeen. I told them how Mr. Aberdeen took me home, how Matthew taught me how to shoot and everything that had happened right up until that night. I even included walking in on Mr. Aberdeen and Matthew, and told them that I was confused and surprised that those two men, who were taking care of me, were such sinners. Nancy's parents just looked at me gravely.

Later that evening Mr. Aberdeen opened his front door to see me with the DeLacey family. Mr. DeLacey had told me I had better go on home and took me back. Mrs. DeLacey, Nancy, and her younger siblings came along for the ride as well. Mr. Aberdeen thanked them for returning me and graciously invited them in. Nancy's father had a very serious expression on his face as he stood in the living room and looked at Mr. Aberdeen and Matthew.

"Young Lloyd here told me that he had witnessed the two of you committing a great mortal sin," he said quietly.

The two gentlemen looked at each other anxiously, faces reddening. They both took a seat and offered a chair to Mr. DeLacey, but he refused.

"However, Lloyd also told us about what happened to his family, about what's going on now, and it makes a lot of sense with everything that's happening. He told us how well Mr. Aberdeen has taken care of him, and out of the generosity of his heart, brought him home and has apparently done him no harm. He told us how Matthew has equally nurtured and cared for him and how he feels very lucky to be alive.

"Now, the preacher can say whatever he wants on Sunday and the Good Book can be interpreted in many different ways by a man, but

I am inclined to agree with Mr. Aberdeen that if there is love, God will not find hate. I believe that you have taken this child in with the goodness of your hearts, and with no ill intent. I have sworn my entire family to secrecy, and we will not tell anybody about your story nor about young Lloyd being here on your farm."

Mr. Aberdeen rose from his seat and crossed the room to shake Mr. DeLacey's hand. "Thank you, sir. I do appreciate it."

I was surprised to see Matthew still sitting in his chair. He didn't get up, he simply looked at Mr. DeLacey, nodded, and managed to mumble a quiet "Thank you, sir," as a tear that had been welling up in his eye finally rolled down his cheek.

I was flabbergasted and dumbfounded. I honestly thought Mr. DeLacey might have had more to say, to do, or even to scold these two men that took me in. But at that moment I realized that maybe sins weren't that simple and that maybe things should be simpler in different ways, that good people could count on each other.

As the DeLacey's turned to walk out the doorway they thanked Mr. Aberdeen and Matthew for their hospitality and Mr. Aberdeen thanked them for bringing me back. I took the opportunity to reach out for a bit more freedom in my young, lonely life.

"Mr. Aberdeen, on account that Nancy and her family now know, will I be able to visit them once in a while?"

Mr. DeLacey looked at Mr. Aberdeen and Mr. Aberdeen looked at him, then back at me.

"Well, if it's alright with Mr. DeLacey, we can work that out every once in a while."

Mr. DeLacey smiled at me. "We will be happy to have you over for a visit any time, son."

"Thank you, sir!" I said, gratefully. I waved goodbye to Nancy and her family and watched them ride off into the night.

Afterward, Mr. Aberdeen sat me down the living room and he and Matthew had a long talk with me.

"Remember when I said there was an incident with a boy at school and my family disowned me for being weak?"

"Yes," I said to Matthew, unsure of what was to come.

"It wasn't because of a fight or bullying. It was because we were in love and my father told me that if I couldn't change, I was a monster and no longer a part of the family or even his son. I tried to change, I really did. That's why I enlisted, to prove to him that I was a real man, or so I thought. We've just figured out that it's okay after all."

"But you're not a monster. Why would he say that?" I asked, indignant.

"Well, just like you said: the preacher said so. Some peoples' beliefs blind them to the fact that love might not always be exactly the way they think it should be." Matthew said.

"That's what we meant, that we still have a long way to go in the United States," said Mr. Aberdeen. "Man may be free in all shapes and colors now, but man is not free to love who they choose without ridicule or persecution. That's why we live out here, because if the people in town knew the true nature of the relationship between Matthew and I, they would likely come here and take everything we own and we'd be lucky to be alive afterwards."

"But that's not fair!" I cried. "Why should they get to take what's yours just because you two love each other?"

"That's a good question," said Matthew, "but some people don't understand that."

"But why do they even care?" I asked. "Why does anyone in town care what you and Mr. Aberdeen are doing if you are in love?"

"That's also a good question, but for some reason some people just haven't come along in a way that we would hope, they haven't advanced intellectually enough to be able to accept anything that is different from what they're used to. So, we have to hide and hope, and keep working towards a better future. Work towards understanding, and hope that we can set an example and eventually be allowed the same freedoms as others. Until then, we have to hide, because if the wrong people find out, the more likely a posse will arrive on our doorstep one day and want to harm us, simply because of whom we choose to love," Mr. Aberdeen explained rationally. I quietly sat for a moment thinking about how I felt and what could happen to them.

"I'm so sorry Mr. Aberdeen, and Matthew," I said remorsefully.

"It's all right, Lloyd," Matthew said. He leaned forward and tousled my hair with his hand. "It's okay now that you're home and everything is fine, and our secret is still safe. I believe Mr. DeLacey is a man of his word and is going to honor his promise not to tell anybody."

THAT NIGHT I LAY AWAKE in bed for quite a while thinking about everything that had happened and everything that I'd done. I just couldn't fathom the world that I lived in, how horrible things could happen to people, how families can be taken by bandits, how good people can be persecuted because they are different, how I almost cost Mr. Aberdeen and Matthew everything that they owned, maybe even their lives. I felt guilt, pity, shame, and the weight of new, adult knowledge, all at once, and I thought about how I wanted the world to be safe for them, for my lost family, for the DeLaceys and myself. I thought about what I could do to change the world we lived in.

FOUR YEARS PASSED IN the blink of an eye; from the night my family was killed until the night the DeLacey's took me home. From then on, I occasionally visited with the DeLacey family. Since we had grown a bit older, Nancy and I had gotten reacquainted and stayed familiar with each other over the next couple of years, through the age where boys and girls begin to see each other differently. By this time, it was customary to be courting the girl that you had affection for. In our case that was a little bit more difficult, seeing as how my existence had to be kept secret. I never fully understood why until I began to visit the DeLacey home regularly and started to hear more about what was going on in town.

Though we weren't courting, Nancy had said that she wasn't courting anyone else. We had some sort of unofficial, unspoken agreement that since I was unable to pursue interest in anyone but her, she was choosing not to court anyone else, either. So, our relationship was as close to courting as it could be under the circumstances. We did enjoy nights on the front porch swing staring at the stars and talking about the things we wanted for the future. We had a little less privacy because it was always in the presence of somebody in her family or my new adoptive one. Occasionally we'd sneak off to the River Glenn oasis, and that was where we had our first kiss, but I was always a gentleman. I had begun to get attached to the DeLacey family, often helping out with chores and things if they needed help. I'd assist in finishing up the chores up at the end of the day when I went to visit Nancy, and that was how I overheard Mr. DeLacey one evening. He was fuming about things that were going on in town.

"Ain't right!" he said slamming his fist on the table.

"Calm down, Percy, it doesn't concern us," his wife said.

"It does concern us, Wilma, it does," Mr. DeLacey said. "Things here have gotten out of control. That slick fellow that came into town, he's cheating people. Daniel, the blacksmith, was having a rough time and that feller, he gave him *half* of what that horse was worth. Daniel was desperate, he needed the money to keep his business afloat. Didn't have a choice. It may not be considered robbery legal-wise, but it's sure as close as it can get, and that new sheriff, he seems to have a lot family around town coming in and taking over businesses. They're pushing decent people out of here."

My interest was piqued. "What new sheriff is that?" I asked Mr. DeLacey.

He hadn't realized I'd heard his outburst and looked at me sideways for a moment, thinking about whether he should respond before conceding to my curiosity.

"The feller that came into town and replaced your pa after he died. Sheriff Behan."

"Behan!" I exclaimed. "Well, that there's what I heard them fellers calling themselves! The ones that killed my pa and ma and burned down the house and all that." I couldn't bring myself to describe the things that had happened to my sister, hesitating for a moment before continuing. A look of horror crossed the DeLacey's faces. Mr. DeLacey looked at me for a long moment.

"Boy, I wish I could say different but that wouldn't surprise me one bit. That clinches it. I'm going to call for a town meeting to get to the bottom and sort out who these snakes are."

"Percy, you'll just bring about more trouble," Wilma warned anxiously.

"No, Wilma," he said. "This is a good town with good people and it's being dragged down by a bad element. We need to stop it now! Come morning we are going to get some answers for this town and set things straight."

Shortly after dinner I said goodbye to the DeLaceys and then gave a long goodbye to Nancy. I climbed up on my mule and she sauntered back home under the cover of darkness. When I arrived home, I explained all of what Mr. DeLacey had wanted me to tell Mr. Sanders and Mr. Aberdeen, and they didn't seem surprised at all.

"There is a lot that we've kept you sheltered from, Lloyd," said Mr. Aberdeen. "I don't like to bring that kind of negativity home, anyway, but there is a lot going on in town that doesn't seem right lately. Hopefully, Mr. DeLacey can help get some answers, but there is really no point in us getting involved. It's just going to bring unneeded attention to us and nobody here can afford that."

The three of us looked back and forth at each other solemnly and quietly, hoping for the best, but I know we all felt deep in the back of our minds that, unfortunately, this wouldn't be the last we heard of it.

Though I shouldn't have been surprised, we all knew something upsetting was happening when, two evenings later, Mr. Aberdeen came galloping home in a rush, infuriated.

"Matthew, Matthew, come help! Hitch up your horse!" Mr. Aberdeen called out hastily.

"What's wrong?" asked Matthew, running out to see him.

"In town, the DeLacey feed mill, it's on fire! We gotta pitch in and try to help put it out," he responded hurriedly as he slowed down his horse.

"What happened?" Matthew asked, his voice rising in alarm.

"Well, they say it was an accident, but I think it's something different. They're saying that bandits rode into town and attacked the DeLaceys! Tried to rob them and, well, Mr. DeLacey, he confronted the sheriff just yesterday and accused him of being a bandit. Now today strangers rode into town, according to the sheriff and his men, and robbed them."

Hearing the commotion, I ran outside. "Are they okay?" I asked Mr. Aberdeen.

"No son, they're not," his voice dropped and he looked at me grimly. "Mr. and Mrs. DeLacey are dead in the street, shot by these alleged bandits, but no one saw what happened. A lot of the townsfolk are afraid to even get involved, and so it's mostly just the DeLacey kids that are trying to put out the flames."

"Well, I'll help, then."

"No, you can't son, stay here. You can't get involved. Matthew can come and help. That shouldn't cause any suspicion, I can just say he is a friend in town visiting," Matthew mounted his horse as Mr. Aberdeen spoke, and they were ready to go.

The two men rode off and I waited anxiously through the supper hour and into the evening, ignoring the hunger gnawing at my belly because of the worry in my head. I thought about riding over to Nancy's but knew there would be no point. She wouldn't be there, anyway, and I wouldn't be able to see her.

It was late in the evening when I heard the familiar hooves of Claudia and Dusty coming back up toward the house. Mr. Aberdeen and Mr. Sanders came in looking filthier than I had ever seen since I'd met them. I could tell that they had tried their best. Soot stained their faces and their clothes, but I knew by the look on their faces that they didn't have anything good to tell me.

"Well, what happened?" I asked impatiently.

"It's gone," Mr. Aberdeen said. "The whole feed mill is gone. We couldn't get the fire out. The flames were reaching up into the sky like a giant red cliff in the desert. Those kids are going to have to rebuild if they ever hope to be able to get the mill running again."

"Well, what about Nancy's ma and pa? What about that crooked sheriff?" I asked, furious with this turn of events. Mr. Sanders and Mr. Aberdeen looked at each other, then back at me.

"The sheriff says that it was unknown bandits and that the cause of this injustice was allowing strangers into our town," Mr. Sanders said. "He is saying that effective immediately they are going to restrict the presence of strangers within the city limits. Those who don't live there will have to check in at the sheriff's station when they arrive in town."

"Well, what about you?" I asked Mr. Aberdeen. "You don't live in town."

"I believe they will be making an exception for me on account of my store being part of the community for so long and me being a familiar face," said Mr. Aberdeen. "But any other stranger coming into town, even Matthew, have to check in at the sheriff's station."

"That ain't fair! That ain't right!" I roared. "That sheriff is an outlaw! He killed people, he killed my ma and pa." Righteously incensed, I held back tears.

"That may be, son, but we can't get involved in this right now. We're both tired and hungry. I am going to cook up something to eat and then we all need to go to bed."

The three of us sat quietly eating a chicken curry Mr. Aberdeen had prepared. Normally, I would've been savoring the sweet and spicy flavors of his exotic cooking that I'd come to love, but that night I brooded in my own thoughts as Mr. Sanders and Mr. Aberdeen did. We ate silently, each of us wrestling with our own demons of emotional trauma. I hadn't been bothered by the nightmares of what happened to my family for a while, but that night I feared their return so much that I spent another night staring wide awake at the ceiling, determined that I would fix things. I would change the world.

The next morning, in my eighteen-year-old's wisdom, I decided I knew exactly how I was going to fix things. Without permission, I had taken down Matthew's pistols from above the door, loaded them, and had taken his gun belt as well. I was all strapped in and ready to go when Mr. Sanders came out of the bedroom.

"What do you think you are doing?"

"I am going to go take care of the sheriff," I said confidently. Mr. Aberdeen soon appeared in the doorway behind Matthew.

"What the hell is all that?"

"I'm going to take care of that crooked outlaw sheriff in town," I said, confidence building. "Someone's got to do it, someone's got to set it right. He's killing and destroying people. He took my family and now he's taken Nancy's."

"Hold on just a minute, boy," Matthew said. "You ain't going to get nowhere with that." Mr. Aberdeen pushed past Matthew through the doorway.

"You're a fool, kid. Don't be a fool. He's got more than a dozen men in town! You riding off like that, you're looking to sign your own death warrant. You'd be committing suicide and be lying dead in the street before you even got to the sheriff," Mr. Aberdeen said. "Only a fool thinks they are going to fix violence with violence. Only a fool thinks they are going to run in and try to shoot their way to justice."

"Well then, maybe I'm a fool, but what else can I do? Something has got to be done. We can't just live in fear."

"Now that's exactly what we can do. We can live in fear or we can die as fools filled with courage." Mr. Aberdeen pointed a finger at me, and quietly said, "We don't have a choice, son." I could tell he was trying to talk me out of my plan. "We've just got to trust that things are going to work out, but we cannot draw unnecessary attention to ourselves and we cannot fix the problems and ills of this world, or even this town, with a gun."

Matthew walked farther into the room and looked at Mr. Aberdeen and then at me. "Gerald is right, son. All three of us could ride into town, and we would just be more bodies in the street. The only way we live, the only way we survive right now, is staying clear of their paths. As long as we stay out of town and don't cause a fuss, we don't raise no attention to ourselves."

"Y'all are cowards!" I screamed at them. Matthew took two long strides forward, our faces only a foot apart.

"You are cruising to be slapped silly for the second time, young man," Matthew said gruffly. I was overcome with emotion. I hated them. Not the men who had raised me, but the men who had killed my family and Nancy's family and taken over the town that I lived in. I was so angry I clenched my teeth, but I couldn't stop the tears from streaming down my face.

"I hate them so much! I want to kill them all myself!" I shrieked. Matthew looked at me sympathetically.

"Son, all you do is carry around hate. You have been carrying around hate in your heart for so long. Hate is gonna take you nowhere. Hate doesn't make anything. If you want to make the world a better place, you've got to do it with the law. If you want to make a difference in the world you stop this kind of thing from happening to other people's families. The best thing you can do, son, is get away from here, go as far as you can."

I was startled at the idea. I looked at Matthew and then Mr. Aberdeen and back at Matthew. Mr. Aberdeen nodded his head in agreement in the background.

"Son, the best thing you can do is leave this town far behind and forget all about it."

"Forget all about it?" I asked, the thought never occurring to me.

"Yes," said Mr. Sanders. "Son, the only thing that lies here for you is heartache and ruin and these men, they have taken more from you than you'd ever deserve, but you stay here and they are going to take even more. Me and Mr. Aberdeen, we both care about you deeply. We want to see you leave this place, we want to see you live happily. We want to see you live well. Seeing that will make us happier than, well, almost anything in the world," Matthew looked at Mr. Aberdeen who nodded in agreement.

Matthew continued, "That won't ever happen if you don't get as far away from this town as possible and take off that gun belt right now."

I hesitated and looked him in the eye. I was as tall as he was now, but he was right. I unbuckled the belt. It slid off and hit the floor and I crumpled into a heap on the kitchen chair. I buried my head in my arms and sobbed. Matthew took a seat next to me.

"Listen, son, here is what I am going to do: I want you to ride to Fort Laramie, eighty miles north of here, that's where I used to be stationed," he said. "I want you to take a letter. I'm going to write a letter of reference for you and you are going to show it to a General Calhoun there. He knows me, and my word will carry weight. You want to make the world a better place, you are going to learn how. You'll do it by serving your country and by being part of the great military forces in the cavalry. They have helped keep the peace across the country. Maybe someday you can find some way to help out things here, but you can't do it now. You've got to live. You've got to survive long enough to make a difference until you can do something here."

"You're sending me away?" I cried in shock. I looked up through tears, feeling hurt on top of everything else that had happened.

"No son, we're setting you free and we're helping you live. We're helping you find some way to be happy, because it just won't happen here."

I looked at Mr. Aberdeen and though I could tell by the expression on his face that he was in agreement with Matthew's words, he couldn't hold back the tears that ran down his cheek.

I thought for a moment and wiped my eyes. "Okay then, I guess I better go re-shoe my nag if I've got that long of a ride ahead of me."

"No," said Mr. Aberdeen. "You leave him here. You're going to take Claudia."

That very day I rode Mr. Aberdeen's beautiful black steed out of town with nothing but a saddle bag full of books and clothes and a letter from Mr. Sanders to help me enlist as a military officer. The two men that had taken care of me since my family's murder told me they wanted me to help protect this nation, and I did just that. Mr. Sander's letter to General Calhoun got me hired on the spot. I served with the American military domestically and in skirmishes abroad.

After five years my duties were complete, at least in that capacity. I had risen up the ranks and earned commendations for marksmanship as well as bravery and courage. I put in a request directly to the White House to enlist as a Federal Marshal to help bring law and order across the country. My service record spoke for itself and the president himself approved my request to operate as a U.S. Marshall, fulfilling bounties and warrants on the most wanted bandits and outlaws within our nation's borders. I even helped swear out warrants on some bandits I kept working hard, gaining experience, finding outlaws and people who had done wrong and took peoples' families or would have taken peoples' families. I kept myself busy all across the mid-western territory for close to two years.

"A WEEK AGO, I RECEIVED a telegram from Mr. Matthew Sanders to let me know that Mr. Gerald Aberdeen had been found dead in the street with a bullet through his head and that's when I decided to come home," the marshal said. His eyes looked up from under the brim of his black hat as a single tear rolled down his cheek. The sheriff and his deputies, the townsfolk, the mayor, and the banker, had been listening to his story.

"See, I grew up ten miles outside of town raised by two proud men, one of them being the Mr. Aberdeen that was running your fine clothing store until his untimely death. My name is Lloyd Church Jr., son of your former sheriff and I'm no stranger to this town. This is where I'm from. Burlton is my home, too."

"Well, that's all very enlightening, sir," Cletus leaned forward on Lloyd's saddle. "But why don't you show me if you've got any proof, any evidence of anything you are claiming right now?"

He held out the lantern as if expecting to inspect evidence.

"You are right, Cletus. It is enlightening. It's always good to know all of the details. Like the fact that I am holding thirty warrants for the Shannon gang and their associates. Namely, one Wilfred Shannon, alias William Behan. One Cletus Shannon, alias Cletus Behan. One James Earl Shannon, alias Jack Behan. One Zebadiah Shannon, alias Zachariah Behan. One George LeClerc, alias Carlyle George, as well as the rest of the Shannon gang and all of their aliases which make up the rest of your deputies in this fine town."

The marshal then turned and gave Cletus a sideways glance. "Like I said, Cletus, I have brought enlightenment and it's always good to know all of the facts. Including the fact that the saddle you are sitting on has its bags full of dynamite."

Marshal Church then drew his pistol from his gun belt so quickly that no one had a chance to react. A bullet fired, causing the gas lamp Cletus held aloft to explode. The fuel sprayed everywhere setting Cletus on fire. He screamed as the saddle underneath him began to burn. The man in black quickly cut his horse free, turned and ran behind the nearest building. A second later the front of the sheriff's station exploded.

Chapter Seven

Smoke and fire filled the streets of Burlton. Cletus crawled on his belly in the dusty street. Smoldering splinters of wood impaled him in several locations of his lower back and legs; the largest one sticking out dangerously close to the base of his spine. He gurgled and groaned, pulling himself through the dirt and ash. He was covered in soot, his clothes were singed, and his open blisters from the flames of the explosion oozed on to the dirt. He made ungodly sounds, pulling one soot-stained chrome-handled revolver from his belt. He waived the gun in the air, uselessly attempting to sight a target and fire. The gentleman in the black bowler hat came striding out from behind a nearby building. Marshal Church roughly stepped on Cletus' gun hand with a crunch.

"Well, Cletus, looks like you've got some shrapnel stuck in you. I'd say you're going to be paralyzed from the waist down, but I think that big piece of wood is probably goin' right through your gut. That means that you're going to be in a lot of pain and it's only going to get worse. You will bleed to death. You're going to die, but it's going to be very slow. If you don't mind though, I'm going to set something right first." He then pulled the chrome-handled pistol out of Cletus' hand. "You don't deserve these guns. They were worn by a man that was much greater than you, but I'll give you your six-shooter back."

With that, Marshal Church snatched the other soot-stained white pistol out of Cletus' belt. The marshal grabbed the revolver from the holster on his hip, then used his free hand to place the two mother-of-pearl handled revolvers into his own gun belt. The marshal quickly spun the chamber of Cletus' pistol, dropped all the bullets on the ground, then put the empty pistol back in Cletus' belt.

"Now, I'm not going to kill you. I'm just going to leave you like this. You'll die and I'll collect the bounty on you later, but I've got too many of your kinfolk to take care of first. In all honesty, a man who sits by and watches horrible acts committed to women and children doesn't deserve to be put out of his misery too quickly, anyway."

Cletus' only response was a glare upward at the marshal and a groan. The marshal reached inside of his jacket and pulled out one folded piece of parchment.

"Here it is. One Cletus Shannon, alias Cletus Behan, wanted on multiple counts of horse thievery, murder, and helping to commit such acts as perpetrated by the Shannon gang." The marshal threw the wanted poster onto Cletus' bloody body. "I will be back for this later. You just rest now. You don't want to get hurt any more than you already are."

Suddenly, there was the sound of a gunshot and a bullet whizzed by Marshal Church lodging itself in the nearby water trough, which had tipped over by the force of the explosion. Marshal Church quickly hustled onto the front porch of the general store next to the sheriff's station. He used one of the large wooden posts as cover to protect himself from the bullets flying at him. Out in the street stood the portly, grizzled form of Sheriff Behan, a.k.a. Zachariah Shannon.

"You sure called down the thunder, boy!" he shouted. "Come out here, you coward! None of what y'all said is true. Now you're killing my nephew and who knows how many other people."

Lloyd Junior looked around and realized that on some level, the sheriff was right. Stunned people, mostly the sheriff's deputies and crooked members of the Shannon gang living under aliases, were stumbling about. Some of them were still in the street, lying in the dirt, a few already dead. No protection was afforded by those tin badges they'd received when they were deputized. People were coughing and staggering around in the smoke. There may have been a couple of innocent people in the crowd, but Lloyd didn't have time to grieve for them when he had an angry outlaw-turned-sheriff firing on him.

"I'm calling you out here, Marshal Church. You come on out and you take your lead pill and let us get back to running this town."

Lloyd popped out from behind the post and fired at the sheriff hitting the dirt near him. The sheriff also took cover, running for the nearest building. Sauntering out of the smoke came the undertaker, Gallant George, looking mighty angry. His black suit was stained with ash and soot, his top hat had rolled in the street. A small gash just below his eye trickled blood. Other than that, Gallant didn't really look too worse for wear.

"Now y'all have done it!" the undertaker howled. The gaunt and lanky man seemed unconcerned about the erupting gun fight and unafraid of the charges that were laid against him by the marshal. "You're a fool. You think you can come in here and change this town. We run this town. We own it. You've been gone too long. I don't care if you're a marshal or not. We're not going to take this—"

George continued to walk forward even after the marshal fired his pistol directly into the man's mouth, which exploded out of the back of his head in a red mist. The man babbled incoherently and took a couple of steps forward, blood spurting from the hole in the back of his head, before he finally collapsed into the street. The marshal stood with his back pressed against a wooden post as wood splintered around his head.

"George Gallant," the marshal proclaimed, "you are wanted dead or alive on several counts of defiling corpses in the states of Arizona, Illinois, and Arkansas, as well three counts of indecent and lewd contact with a minor, three counts of rape, seven counts of murder across this nation and general horse thievery. I do believe that you have now had your sentence carried out."

The marshal looked out into the street and saw that the sheriff had disappeared. Marshal Church stepped out into the street and pulled George's wanted poster out of his jacket. Unfolding the paper, he dropped it on the undertaker's corpse.

"And I don't waste my time listening to rapists and necrophiles."

A moment later there was a scuffling as three of Sheriff Behan's deputies came running out of an alley between buildings. Each of the deputies leveled a pistol at the avenging lawman. The marshal used both hands on one gun, cocking the hammer with one hand and pulling the trigger with the other firing off several shots. The gunfire took out all three men, each with a single bullet, before they even had a chance to aim. The marshal walked into the center of the street and called out in front of the town so that they could all hear him:

"People of Burlton, you've been oppressed by an outlaw gang posing as lawmen and business people for fifteen years. Every single one of these men has a warrant for their arrest and I am here to serve those warrants, dead or alive. I am an authorized U.S. Federal Marshal and I have the power to deputize any person brave enough to stand with me against these outlaws. These are the men that have been stealing your livelihoods and profiting from your deaths for fifteen years. If y'all are brave enough to stand with me, join me now and I assure you, you will be on the side of the law and of the righteous."

The door of McCoolie's drugstore burst open. McCoolie himself stood there with a long, double-barreled shotgun. The gun erupted giving Marshal Church barely enough time to get out of the way.

"You're dead man, marshal!" McCoolie screamed. "You can't fight these people! They're in charge. You should've found a way to profit from them like I did, but now you're just going to die and everything's going to go back to the way we want it."

A shot rang through the air. McCoolie had leveled his gun but it hadn't gone off. He slowly dropped to his knees as a dark red patch began to grow on his chest. Confused, he looked to the other end of the street as blood bubbled over his lips. As the smoke cleared, Sam the saloon owner appeared on the front stoop of his establishment, both barrels of his shotgun releasing wisps of smoke. The doctor fell flat on his face and uttered his last breath.

"You Shannon's talk too damn much!" Sam hollered and looked over at the marshal. "You are going to deputize me, right? So, that was legal, right?"

The marshal grinned at Sam.

"Welcome to the gunfight, deputy. Let's take back your town."

"Damn straight!" Sam shouted. The marshal crawled into the street, pulled a tin star off one of the dead lawmen, and tossed it to Sam.

Chapter Eight

S am grabbed the tin star and slipped it into his vest pocket, not having time to pin it on, then raised his shotgun again. For a moment, the marshal thought Sam was leveling it at the marshal himself, but Sam hoisted the gun higher and fired. Two of Behan's deputies had been sneaking up on the roof of the porch that the marshal was hiding under. Two bodies fell to the ground, dead in the street.

"Much obliged, deputy!" the marshal shouted out.

"Not at all, marshal," Sam replied.

The two men reloaded their weapons. Sam took that moment to pin the star onto his chest and they walked into the middle of the street.

"Do you accept the sworn duties of a deputized official in the capacity of serving federal warrants on the criminals of the Shannon, alias, Behan family?"

"Well, I certainly do, marshal," Sam said seriously.

"And you swear to uphold the word and the letter of the law, and that you shall not execute any warrant on said felons unless their identity is without question?"

"Sure, do marshal."

"Welcome, deputy!" Marshal Church said shaking Sam's hand.

Sam reloaded his shotgun and fired at another man wearing the same kind of star that he had on. The man had been creeping up from behind the corner of the building. Marshal Church fired two rounds through the nearby window of a house and an outlaw, one of the younger Shannon-turned-Behan's, came tumbling out into the street and fell face down. All was quiet for a moment before the outlaws regrouped, encamping behind an overturned hay wagon. The gunfire erupted fiercely. Earlier, the street had been full of people running and coughing and taking cover. Now, the streets were full of lead. Bullets were flying everywhere and seemed to come from all directions, aimed at the marshal and his new deputy. They took cover as wood and glass splintered all around them

"You know marshal, maybe I should rethink this whole idea. Maybe the Behan's bein' in charge ain't so bad." The marshal glared at him and Sam glanced back with a grin. "I'm just kidding, these guys are assholes."

Sam then fired a shot over the railing of a veranda that was offering some cover. Bullets whizzed by and shattered more wood and glass. The men kept firing back, hoping for a chance to find cover. They were getting low on ammunition and the bullets seemed to keep raining down on them for minutes at a time. The marshal and his deputy began to doubt their righteous mission was going to be successful. The expression on both men's faces said that maybe they had gotten in over their heads. Marshal Church realized he was running low on ammunition and needed to reload. The commotion of the gunfire coming from behind them distracted them long enough for a figure to approach. They looked up and saw the banker, Ezekiel George, staring down at them. He had two guns drawn in his hands and pointed them at the lawmen. The crooked outlaw-turned-financier grinned.

"I bet you didn't think it was going to be the banker that took your digits, did you?"

The banker cocked the hammers on his pistols, and leveled them at the two men but suddenly two wounds erupted on his own chest synchronized with the sound of gunfire. The wounds blossomed and splattered blood on either side of him. The man dropped to his knees in wide-eyed confusion. From around the next building through a cloud of smoke stepped an old Southern gentleman, his bushy orange mustache turning white with age. Next to him, a pale horse had been hitched. The horse didn't seem to mind the sound of the gunfire from the two smoking pistols. Matthew Sanders walked slowly toward the three men, eyes locked on the dying man whose hands no longer had the strength to hold his pistols. Matthew glared down at Ezekiel George.

"It was you, I know it was," he hissed.

"What was?" the banker moaned, bleeding from his chest.

"You put a bullet in the head of the man I loved," he said.

For a moment, all the memories of the good times that Matthew had with Gerald flashed through his mind. Memories of looking at the stars in the swing, of cuddling by the fireplace, of dancing in the kitchen while making dinner, of sharing a picnic in the grass, rushed agonizingly through his mind.

"How did you know?" the banker gasped with his last breaths.

"You are wearing his vest," Sanders responded through clenched teeth. Matthew then fired a bullet into the man's head. The war veteran turned to face the boy he'd helped raise, now a grown man.

"When I heard about the marshal that had come into town yesterday and caused an uproar, I knew it was you," he said, as tears of pride welled up in his eyes. Lloyd looked back at Matthew with his eyes brimming, too.

"I knew you would," Lloyd smiled weakly.

"Why didn't you stop by the house? Why didn't you come in and tell me you were in town?" Sanders asked.

"Because I needed to do this . . ." said the marshal, "and I knew you would try to talk me

out of it."

"Damn fool," Sanders said. "Of course I would've tried to talk you out of it!" He held his guns as if to show them to the younger man. "These guns," he sobbed, tears now rushing down his face like a river, "they sat in the same place over that door for seven years. I hadn't touched them in seven years, because I knew Gerald didn't like them and he didn't want them there. He never wanted me to use them. So, the first time I held these guns in seven years—" Matthew could no longer speak as emotion began to choke him. Marshal Church now wept openly, too.

"I'm sorry I let you down, Matthew," he said through his tears.

"You didn't let me down, you damn fool," he said. "Get the ammo out of his guns . . ." Matthew gestured toward the dead banker, "and let's kill these sons of bitches."

Retired General Matthew Sanders then leaned over the railing of the veranda and began to fire, giving Sam and Marshal Church enough cover to reload their weapons. The gunfire began to die down; at first it seemed because possibly the enemy needed to reload. When Marshal Church peeked into the street he saw at least ten more dead men than there had been before. Sam poked his head up and looked, too.

"Holy Jesus! There are more dead guys than bullets you fired!" Sam exclaimed.

"I see you haven't lost the touch," chuckled Marshal Church.

"Ain't no rust on me, boy," Sanders responded smugly.

"Much obliged for your help there, sir," Sam said, "and don't worry, I heard your story, and I don't have any problem with you and your . . . well, you know, likin' fellas."

"Well, that's good," Sanders responded sarcastically, "I was really concerned about that while I was saving your life and all."

"No, no. No disrespect meant, sir," Sam said apologetically. "I got an uncle I once caught wearing a ladies' petticoat. Never had a problem with him. I never said a word to anybody else, and never treated him any different. He was family."

"Mighty big of you, sir," Sanders said cynically.

"Yeah, we remain friends. He actually gave me the money to start up my saloon here."

"Oh, he did that, did he? So you'd keep quiet?" Matthew asked, starting to get upset.

"No, no. He did that as a thank you. I helped him get a job at the bordello over there."

Matthew looked over to the upper balcony where Sam pointed, to a very hairy-lipped woman in a corset and frilly gown who looked down and waved at them.

"I know how to keep a secret. Whether he does or not, I don't know. His clients sure do, though. So, I'm totally fine with all that, just so you know. You want to wear a lady's dress, you go right ahead."

"I don't wear dresses," said Sanders severely. "I'm a veteran of the United States Army."

"Sorry, sir. No offense meant."

"Focus on the enemies before I start to take offense," said Sanders.

A grinning Marshal Church interrupted the awkward exchange by looking at the man that helped raise him.

"Are you ready to go in and close some of these bastards down?" he asked.

"More than ready," Sanders replied, glad to change the subject.

The three men strolled into the street firing in different directions, offering each other cover and taking out all hostile, fraudulent lawmen that presented any danger.

Chapter Nine

The three men strolled down the street firing at threats on rooftops and porches, taking out the corrupt deputies that had attached themselves to the Shannon gang.

Just like earlier, there was a sudden resurgence. Bullets began to fly in their direction. The men took shelter behind some gallows that had been erected in the middle of the street. The marshal looked at the other two men.

"Somehow, I get the feeling that they hadn't intended to let me leave," Marshal Church said as he shifted his gaze to the gallows above them, ropes dangling like a bad omen.

"There's always an excuse for hanging these days," said Sam. They looked around trying to determine the number of enemies that were potentially hiding in the streets.

"We got too much for us to handle all at once," the marshal said. "We're going to need to spread out and draw some of these criminals outta hiding." Sanders looked at them thoughtfully.

"We should split up."

"Well, I think that's a clever idea," the marshal said, but Sam looked puzzled.

"Are you sure? I mean, ain't we stronger together?"

"No doubt, Sam," the marshal said, "but right now, we are one big target too easy to hit all together. We got too many enemies out there. If we can lure some of them out individually, it should improve our chances when we get into a back-to-back firefight again."

"I'm with you, marshal, whatever you say," Matthew said.

"Me, too," agreed Sam, a bit reluctantly.

"Okay, we're going to split up," the marshal said as Matthew Sanders gestured to the steeple in the distance.

"I'll take the church."

The marshal peered over the top of the gallows. "I've got some unfinished business at the bordello."

"I'm sure you do," chuckled Sam.

"Not like that, Sam," the marshal said with a sly grin.

"Well, since you're taking the bordello, I'm going to go and make sure that none of the outlaws are takin' off with those horses," Sam motioned to the horse pen in the distance.

"That's a great idea, Sam," said Marshal Church.

"We need to use the chaos of all this gunfire to sneak away," said Sam confidently. Retired General Sanders gave the bartender a sideways glance.

"That's the smartest thing I've heard you say yet!" Sanders said, amused. Sam was about to take offense for a moment, then decided against it.

"I have my moments."

Through the dust, smoke, and gunfire, Matthew Sanders slowly crept toward the church. He could hear a commotion inside and the murmurs of a voice giving instructions.

"Now, stay calm," it said, "this is the house of the Lord and we shall keep away from any evil goings on. The Lord himself will protect you, as he protects me, from these devils coming in from outside of our fair town." Matthew had heard enough and kicked in the front doors of the church.

"Bullshit, he will!" yelled Matthew. The retired soldier found himself in front of a group of frightened women and children that had taken shelter.

"Actually, let me reword that."

The phony pastor, Josiah Shannon posing as Josiah Behan, had assembled a number of children around him. Small boys and girls, some as young as three and on up to about twelve years of age, huddled in a mass behind the pastor in front of a giant carving of Jesus. The pastor turned to face Matthew Sanders.

"This is the house of the Lord and you do not belong here! We are not part of your fight." Matthew looked at the preacher skeptically.

"Is that so?"

"It is so, and the righteousness of the truth and the Lord shall prevail," Josiah said piously. Matthew fired a bullet into the ceiling.

"Shut the hell up, 'Pastor' Behan," Matthew ordered. The elderly southern gentleman then looked at the terrified children.

"I want to ask you something." Matthew knelt down so as not too look so scary to the children.

"Is there any single one of you . . . raise your hand now . . . is there a single one of you here that has *not* been made to feel uncomfortable by this man?" He pointed to the pastor with his gun. "To have *not* had questionable things suggested to you by this man, never been abused or touched by this man? If any of you can speak up and say he has not harmed you or made you feel uncomfortable in some way, raise your hand." The children just stared at the man silently.

"I'm telling you," he continued, "I will not shoot your pastor if a single one of you can tell me he has not harmed you in any way."

The children looked nervously at each other, at the pastor—who glared at them in warning—and then back at the orange-mustached man. As the truth of the situation began to sink in with the mothers sitting in the pews, some began to weep in realization; none of the children had denied the allegations.

"Well, they don't know what you're talking about," said the phony pastor anxiously. "They don't know any better."

"All right kids, if you love your pastor and you think that he isn't ever going to harm you or defile you in any way, then stay right where you are. Otherwise, you might want to move out of the way."

The children looked at each other and parted like the Red Sea, leaving the walkway between the pews nothing but open space between the aged veteran and the phony pastor.

"You think you've proved anything?" Josiah began to shout, "you think you've got righteousness on your side? You're the one that's going to burn in hell. I'm on the side of the Lord, you fa—"

The pastor's slur was interrupted by the sound of two gunshots. Eyes widening, he looked down at two smoking holes in his stomach. The bullets hit dead center through the large embroidered golden cross on his robe. The holes oozed smoke and quickly began to turn red. The pastor made a gurgling noise, turned around and attempted to flee, but had trouble keeping his legs underneath him. Instead, he crawled toward the giant sculpture of Jesus with its hands reaching for the sky. The pastor was holding on to the carved wooden feet.

"I am sorry for what I've done, Lord. Please accept my confession. Let me die with my soul cleansed."

Before Josiah could get out another word, Matthew shot the metal hinge bolts on the ceiling that held the sculpture in place, causing it to topple over and flatten the preacher.

The children that had been squeezing themselves into the pews slowly moved back to the walkway. They stared at the pastor. One child stepped forward and looked at Matthew earnestly.

"Thank you, sir. Thank you so much."

Then several children behind him began kicking the pastor's corpse and spitting on it. Matthew looked at the child who had spoken, and then at the rest of them.

"Lord works in mysterious ways, boy. You're very welcome."

As mothers rushed comfort their children, Matthew Sanders turned around and walked out of the church.

Chapter Ten

S am strolled towards the horse pen at the end of the street. There, he saw the man he knew as Carlyle George; local realtor and horse peddler. George was hurriedly grabbing supplies and valuables from his home nearby and packing them onto a saddle that had been thrown over the magnificent black steed that Marshal Church had ridden into town.

"Y'all wouldn't be skipping town, now would you, Mr. George?" Sam asked.

"What is it to you, rummy?" George retorted without interrupting the pace of his packing. "Look at this town. Everything's going to hell."

"Well, it seems to me that there was a warrant out for your arrest, and well, I'm a deputy now."

"Oh, you're a deputy now?" Carlisle George replied. "Well, I'm sorry. Here, there must be a misunderstanding," the man raised his arms in mock surrender, "but if you need to take me in and question me, Deputy Barkeep, you go ahead," he said sarcastically. Then, suddenly, flicking his wrist, a small pistol on the end of an extractor arm in his sleeve popped out and placed a small gun in his hand. "Of course, looks like I got the drop on you now," George boasted.

In response, Sam's gun fired, blasting through the chest of the man.

"These guys really do talk too much," Sam exclaimed as he took furtive steps towards the man to verify that he was deceased.

Seconds later, Sam's chest exploded with pain. A bullet ripped through his shoulder causing him to fall to the ground. He rolled over to see James Shannon, the extortionist insurance salesman, drawing upon him. The man chuckled and walked over to him. Standing above Sam in the street, he grinned and pointed a pistol in the dead center of the bartender's face. Sam struggled to get ahold of his shotgun, but knew he wouldn't have time to fire off a round before the extortionist could fire.

Sam stared down the barrel of James Shannon's pistol and noticed that the chamber of his revolver showed several empty spots; likely from the firefight that had been going on in the street. The gloating insurance salesman looked down at Sam.

"Looks like you should have bought some more insurance." The man squeezed the trigger and his gun responded with an audible *click*. Sam grinned and gripped his shotgun, raising it toward the surprised gang member.

"Looks like you should have bought more bullets." Sam emptied the second barrel of his shotgun into James Shannon's stomach, causing him to stumble backward and fall dead in the street.

"How . . . how in the hell did y'all take over this town when y'all are so stupid?" The saloon owner pulled himself up, nursing his shoulder and looked at the black steed tied to the post in front of him.

Chapter Eleven

Federal Marshal Lloyd Church Jr. took a deep breath and walked through the doors of the bordello. Women in all manner of undress were cowering in corners and hiding behind anything that could offer some cover. In a closet under the back stairs, the marshal heard a rustling and murmur of voices. A young man had ducked into the closet along with the Madam Drusilla Behan. The young man stood beside her, pistol drawn in one hand, the other hand gently stroking her belly.

"Oh, Mama," he said. "I can't stay back here, I can't. There's no way that I'm going to let him kill our kin. He can't take away the only family we have or this baby we've made together."

"No, Junior, you need to be patient. My daddy is going to take care of all this. He's going to send that man home in a casket, we just need to stay out of the way and hide until it's taken care of."

"Oh, you don't believe that, do you? A man has got to act! Your dad is an idiot. I'm going to go take care of this myself."

"Now you hush your mouth, you know he's your daddy, too."

"I don't care," the eager young man said. "I'm going to go take care of this marshal all on my own!"

The young man burst forth from the closet and screamed out.

"You're gonna die, marshal!"

The marshal, who had been approaching the closet since he entered the bordello, simply fired several bullets directly through the young man as he neared the staircase. The man fell without firing a single shot whatsoever from his pistol. He curled up on the floor whimpering before he died.

The marshal made his way up the stairs to the chamber of Nancy DeLacey and with one kick bashed the door in while reloading his pistol. The woman inside screamed out in fright. Then she recognized the marshal and jumped up, angry.

"What are you doing back here?" she hissed as she closed the door.

"Come here to make things right and help you get outta here." Nancy looked at him, flabbergasted.

"This isn't a penny novel," she said nastily. "Just because you think you can even the score for your parents doesn't mean I'm gonna ride off with you into the sunset."

"Why not, Nancy? Come on! Now, I'm willing to overlook that you became a lady of the night and give you a better life."

"I'm doing well enough to provide for myself," Nancy responded. "You don't get to just *have* me."

The marshal stood there, dumbfounded. Suddenly the door was kicked in again. The young man hadn't bled to death downstairs after all. Nursing a wound in his chest, he fired his gun wildly around the room shattering the window. The marshal turned around and fired once causing the man to stumble backward and break through the railing, falling down to the story below.

"You won't come with me?" the marshal asked, turning back to her in disbelief.

"No, I'm doing fine on my own," she said spitefully.

"All right, then," the marshal turned to leave and found himself face to face with a large, angry, pregnant Drusilla Behan in the doorway.

"You son of a bitch, you killed my boy and my baby's daddy!"

"At the same time?" the marshal asked in surprise. Hearing that, she screamed and attacked him, her claw-like nails grabbed at his face and scratched him up.

"I don't intend to fire on a lady," said the marshal trying to hold her off.

"Won't find no ladies here!" screamed Drusilla.

She grabbed the coat rack and swung it at him. The marshal dodged it once and dodged it again. Her the third attempt connected with his jaw which caused him to reel back and left his head spinning. She whirled around for another hit but the marshal dodged it and leaned forward, and against his better instincts, punched the woman in the face knocking her sideways over the dresser. She slumped to the floor, seemingly unconscious.

"Well, I guess my job here is done," he said to Nancy. "Sorry to have disrupted your day," the marshal replaced his hat, made his way through the door, and walked past the broken railing down the hallway.

Behind him, Drusilla swiftly emerged from the room white-hot angry and screeching. Instead of chasing after him, she reached inside her petticoat and pulled out a small pistol she had tucked under her breasts and leveled it at the back of the marshal's head. Unexpectedly Nancy came out the door, slapped Drusilla, and knocked the pistol from her hand.

"Why, you little hussy!" Drusilla shouted.

She swung around and punched Nancy. Nancy stopped and looked at her for a moment, then returned the punch knocking Drusilla unconscious. Her body slumped sideways and backward falling through the open railing. She fell to the floor below with a heavy thud, on top of the corpse of her son who had impregnated her. The marshal watched the scene in shocked astonishment then hurried down the stairs in time to see the final light of life leave Drusilla's eyes. A pool of blood started growing around the pair as the marshal stared at the macabre scene. Nancy joined him and he looked over his shoulder at her.

"I don't even know what to call this," he mumbled to her. Nancy grabbed a revolver out of the dead man's belt.

"Let's get out of here," she said urgently. The marshal drew a warrant from his coat and tossed it on Drusilla's body.

"Drusilla Behan, you are wanted on four counts of cattle rustling and three counts of lewd and lascivious conduct," he declared. Then the marshal and Nancy DeLacey turned and hurried out of the bordello.

.

Chapter Twelve

The marshal and his three new deputies: the retired general, a prostitute and a saloon owner, all met in the center of a dusty street. Sam, nursing a bullet wound in his shoulder, was pulling the bridle on Claudette.

"Much obliged that you retrieved my horse," the marshal said to Sam.

"Well, I would have ridden it over but I seem to be having a bit of trouble getting up in the saddle myself," he said gesturing at his wound.

"Well, I am sorry, Sam. I do rightly appreciate you going through all the trouble," Marshal Church said apologetically.

"I closed down that realtor and the insurance salesman so we are even on those counts, but you should know it looks like some of them horses have been taken out, and I think some of them may have gotten away."

The marshal chuckled, "Do you, Matthew Sanders, and you, Miss Nancy DeLacey, promise to uphold the law and serve these federal warrants for which I have deputized you to assist in?"

"Yeah, we get it," said Nancy. "Blah, blah, blah. I agree."

"Matthew?"

"Me too," Matthew said. Marshal Church pinned a star on each of their chests.

"Matthew, you go get Dusty. We're going to hunt the rest of these Behans down." Marshal Church looked at Nancy and Sam. "You two stay here and close in on any stragglers. Matthew and I are going to chase down the Shannon patriarchs." With that, Matthew and Marshal

Church rode side by side down the dusty street and out of town. Nancy glanced at Sam.

"Well, what are we supposed to do now?"

"Keep shooting outlaws, I guess?" Sam said uncertainly.

"Yeah, don't mind us, fellas," said Nancy. "You guys just get the horses and leave, and we'll just stay here without horses and just, you know, shoot bad guys and stuff."

The two crouched behind a nearby hay wagon.

"Nice to see that you could join us, Nancy," whispered Sam.

"Nice to see that you were able to find a backbone, Sam," Nancy whispered back.

"Well, it is one of my flaws," Sam replied.

The barkeep then popped up, fired off a shot at a would-be assassin trying to crawl up on a roof nearby. The two hunkered down and exchanged jibes while firing off at the few remaining outlaws still hiding in town.

Meanwhile, Matthew and Lloyd were galloping at full speed following a cloud of dust heading out into the desert. They raced for several miles until the cloud stopped. Those pursued on horseback had dismounted at the familiar River Glenn oasis. Matthew and Lloyd slowly ambled up on their horses to the front of the oasis. There stood the four men: the mayor, the landlord, the judge and the sheriff. Marshal Church looked at them as he dismounted his horse.

"Zachariah, Wilfred, Robert, and Allister Shannon. Founders of the Shannon gang now going by the alias' of Behan, all respectively, of course, though you may not be respectable," said the marshal. "Looks like you got tired of running."

"Oh, we weren't running," said Sheriff Zachariah Behan confidently. "We're letting the horses get a good drink. See, we operate this town and we thought of running, but decided instead we'd rather just kill you and go back to town. Things will get back to the way they've been. I think the people will fall back in line once they see us drag a pair of 'heroes' into town as corpses."

"That's an interesting theory," said the marshal.

"Not that you can prove any of these charges that you're hunting us down for," the sheriff replied as he spat on the ground.

"Well, you know what? Maybe I got this wrong," said the marshal. "Maybe I can hear some testimonies. You know, we'll have a trial right here on the spot and maybe I'll let you guys go free and clear and just tear up these warrants. They could be mistakes. So, tell me your side of the story, fellas. What are we missing?" Allister Behan stepped forward arrogantly.

"I am a respectable mayor of this community and these charges have not been thoroughly proven. In fact, I don't believe there is any evi—"

The mayor was interrupted by the sound of a gunshot. A bullet shot through his throat from a gun the marshal had quickly drawn from his hip and smoke floated up from the barrel. The man fell to his knees, choking on blood spluttering from both his mouth and the hole in his throat.

"I don't listen to the testimony of rapists in my courtroom," said the marshal angrily. "Unlike your judge, right?"

"Mayor Allister Behan, a.k.a. Allister Shannon, I have filled your warrant on the count of rape and murder of one Camille Church."

"Now just hold on, gentlemen," said the judge cordially. "I mean, we are still outnumbering you three to two. Maybe we can come to some sort of agreement, some sort of truce." The judge reached into a pocket but before he could pull the gun he had been attempting to grab, two shots were fired through his chest from the pistols of Matthew Sanders, both drawn and fired at the same time. The outlaw stumbled and fell backward into the pond. Air escaped his lungs as he struggled but he was only able to roll over and drown as his blood slowly turned the water red.

"Looks like the odds are even now," said Sanders.

"Well, on top of that, sir, I can't help but add another charge of horse thievery," Marshal Church said. The fugitives' steeds lapped the cool liquid from the pool, oblivious to the fact that a dead man was floating in it.

"Oh, yeah, and how's that, son?" the sheriff asked.

"Well, your nag there, it's actually my nag. And it was ridden by one Mr. Aberdeen, who allegedly committed suicide after daring to challenge your family member who is now going to need to be put in the ground. I don't know how you're going to do that; the undertaker's dead, too, I don't know if you caught that. Regardless, it's got my brand on it, and 'round these parts, horse thievery itself is punishable by hanging."

"Now, wait just a minute."

"No, I think you should wait a minute. You should wait a minute and think about everything you've done to people and tell me why you don't think you deserve your punishment." Landlord Wilfred Shannon and the bogus Sheriff Zachariah Shannon stood before the two men in the desert.

The four glared at each other, eyes narrowed, looking back and forth. The men were on edge; their anxiety grew with the heat. Neither of the criminals dared to speak a word and neither of the lawmen dared to waste a word, concerned about losing even a split second.

A moment later the dry Arizona desert air rang with the sound of multiple gunshots. Within seconds the two elderly outlaws writhed in agony on the desert floor, each with a bullet through their gun hands, moaning and sobbing. Marshal Church stood before the men.

"I serve my warrants on you, Zachariah Shannon, alias Zachariah Behan, and William Shannon, alias Wilfred Behan. You are the patriarchs of the Shannon gang and you have committed crimes across the United States of America. You are wanted in seven states; you have multiple counts of murder, of theft, of rape, of horse wrangling against you, and you killed my family. Now the law is going to see that you receive your proper sentence." Zachariah Behan looked up at the young man.

"Go ahead and do it. End me," he said quietly.

"You will face judgement, sir." Marshal Church grabbed two ropes from the saddle bag on Matthew's horse and bound the injured wrists of both men.

Matthew tied the other end of the rope attached to Wilfred Behan to the bullhorn on his saddle. Marshal Lloyd Church Jr. likewise tied Zachariah Shannon, alias Zachariah Behan, to the bullhorn of his saddle. The men's horses sauntered through the desert back toward town, their owners sitting tall in the saddle and the fugitives they had captured straggling behind, tethered to ropes.

Chapter Thirteen

Any remaining loyalists of the Shannon-turned-Behan gang had either turned tail and gotten out of town or been shot by a strange duo of deputies; the injured saloon owner and the prostitute. The fire had subsided at the sheriff's station but the smoke and dust clouds still filled the streets from all the commotion. Through the haze the marshal and his adoptive father—now a deputy—rode into town on their horses, pulling the fugitive gangsters into town. The lawmen kept their horses going just slow enough so the men being dragged along on the ropes had to keep walking. But it looked like the criminal sheriff must have tripped once or twice since the knees of his pants were torn and he was bleeding.

As they walked into town, curious townsfolk began to pop out of the windows and doors. A man came out on his front porch and watched in disbelief.

"Thank God! Thank God you did it, you got them, you actually got them!" The man stammered enthusiastically. "You got them all."

Excited townspeople began to come out of hiding. Those that hadn't felt safe in their own homes for years began to flood the streets. The fugitives tied to the saddles glared at the townsfolk as the people tipped their hats to the marshal.

"Thank you, marshal," said another thrilled townsperson, "thank you, Marshal Church!"

The procession went on. The two men walked their prisoners past the ruined sheriff's station to the gallows at the end of the street. The marshal dismounted his horse and untied his fugitives. Holding on the ends of the ropes he walked up to the gallows erected.

"Good people of Burlton," the marshal began, "the Shannon gang has oppressed you for a long time now. Some of you may not even remember what it was like when Burlton was a happy and decent place, but it was once and I would ask you to make it so again. These men have been found guilty of crimes against people and animals in seven states Under my authority they are going to receive punishment for those crimes. They are wanted dead or alive, considering the crimes and the oppression they have committed and inflicted upon you, and for the murder of Sheriff Lloyd Church and his family. Along with that, for the murder of one Mr. Gerald Aberdeen, the murder of Percy and Wilma DeLacey, and the murders of countless other townsfolk. I believe the best way to serve this warrant is to hang them by the neck until they are dead."

With that proclamation, the sheriff and his landlord brother suddenly found new energy. They began to struggle and tried to free themselves from the marshal's grip. In response, Matthew Sanders strode up to them and pressed a six shooter into the nose of each one.

"Don't you move, you yellow pieces of shit," he snarled.

The marshal continued, "However, it's not for me to decide. I'm going to leave it up to the people of Burlton and your new sheriff because I'm not going to stay. I still have plenty of work to do serving warrants as a representative of the president of the United States." A gasp of disappointment spread across the crowd. "But I urge you to support me in appointing a new, temporary sheriff until such time as your community can organize an election to make it official. Retired General Matthew Sanders." Matthew looked at the young man he'd raised in surprise.

"Mr. Sanders," the marshal continued, "I do believe you would be the best choice to help keep the peace in this town until such time as

Burlton is able to go back to the peaceful community that it once was."
Before Matthew could respond a cheer came from the crowd.

"Three cheers for Sheriff Sanders! Hip hip, hooray! Hip hip, hooray! Hip hip, hooray!"

"Can I still be deputy?" asked Sam, hand raised. The marshal looked at his adoptive father.

"Well, sure Sam . . . part-time," the newly appointed sheriff said, "around running your saloon."

"It's an honor, sir!" Sam shouted back smiling.

The marshal continued, "Like I said, I want to leave this decision up to the people of Burlton and your new sheriff. Sheriff, what do you say? Do I pick these two up, take them to Fort Laramie and have them judged in a hearing there, or do we hang them right now?"

The Southern gentleman beheld the criminals staring back at him in desperation. Then Matthew looked down at the ground and thought for a moment of all the good times he had shared with a British gentleman he had met while serving his country. And how he never would again.

"Hang 'em," he said. The crowd cheered.

Moments later the two fugitives stood on top of a trapdoor. Ropes were placed around their necks, the other end fastened securely around the beam overhead. Nancy DeLacey approached the marshal.

"So, you're not staying?" she asked with a hint of disappointment in her voice.

"No, I can't stay. It's my sworn duty to fill out these warrants. I have to report back to the Capitol to update them on my progress and get a new list of wanted felons across the country."

"Well," she said, "that's a shame."

"Why is that?" the marshal asked.

"You might've been able to have me after all," she said flirtatiously. He smiled, leaned forward, and kissed her passionately.

"You might like things in Washington," he said.

"Oh yeah?" she asked, "what do they have there?"

"Everything," he said.

"Well then," she smiled, "I guess I'll come along."

"You need to go and pack your bags?" he asked.

"Shoot, no," she said, "you just told me, they got everything there." With that, she extended her hand and the marshal helped her climb into the saddle and settle on the back of Claudette. "Besides, you just might need to keep someone else around as a deputy to help you out with those warrants."

"Absolutely not!" the Marshal exclaimed.

"I don't remember asking you, marshal," Nancy said with a laugh.

Lloyd Church Jr. turned and looked at the orange-haired gentleman standing on the gallows holding the warrants that he had given him.

Matthew loudly proclaimed, "One Zachariah Shannon, alias Zachariah Behan, you have been charged and found guilty of the murder of Sheriff Lloyd Church, his wife and his daughter as well as impersonating a man of law, as well as several counts of horse thievery, as well as lewd conduct. As well as, oh shit! I'm not going to read all these charges!" Matthew then turned to the other fugitive. "William Shannon, alias Wilfred Behan, you're charged with all the same things. Have fun in hell."

He then pushed a lever which opened the trap doors and both men fell writhing and wiggling, gagging and clawing at their ropes, until the life left their eyes, the struggle left their bodies, and the feces left their bowels and ran down their legs.

The marshal and Nancy turned and smiled, giving a nod and a wave to Matthew Sanders and Sam O'Hara in succession. The new sheriff waved and smiled at the couple, watching them as they rode off down the dusty street into the open desert and off into the sunset.

The End

Don't miss out!

Visit the website below and you can sign up to receive emails whenever Mike Gagnon publishes a new book. There's no charge and no obligation.

https://books2read.com/r/B-A-RBQB-SXZU

BOOKS 2 READ

Connecting independent readers to independent writers.

Also by Mike Gagnon

Orlok
Orlok

Standalone
Skidsville
The Island of Dr. Morose
The Illusion of Freedom
A Letter to the Middle East
A Western Gentleman
Project Magenta

Watch for more at www.mikegagnon.ca.

About the Author

Mike Gagnon is an author living in the Niagara Region of Canada.

He has been a professional writer and comic creator since 2003. He has written, illustrated and edited hundreds of books, articles and graphic novels.

Mike has worked for publishers of all sizes, from Marvel Comics to many small press publishers.

For more info visit: www.mikegagnon.ca

Read more at www.mikegagnon.ca.